# A DOG'S TALE

## Sparky Rescues The Prestons

# A DOG'S TALE
## Sparky Rescues The Prestons

# DAN GRUNWALD

THREE 444s PUBLISHING

Three 444s Publishing
Ventura, Iowa

www.sparkyrescuestheprestons.com

ISBN: 978-0-6929792-3-5

*To my wife Jude: Without your help and support,*
*I never would have completed this project.*

*To my parents: For always being a good example.*

# 1

Here it was, 3:45 in the afternoon. And it was not good! In fact, it was nine-year-old Todd Preston's least favorite time on any given school day. The fourth grader had been home less than 10 minutes when his older brother Michael slammed his way through the back door. He was a sophomore at Parkerville High School, *the big school*, and took every opportunity to remind Todd that he was here on earth for only one reason... Michael's entertainment. At least that's the way it seemed to Todd, who jumped every time he heard the sound of Michael's books smack down on the kitchen counter.

"What's wrong with you, Toad?" Michael smirked, delighting in Todd's discomfort.

"Shut up, Michael! Mom told you not to call me that!"

"Well... Mom's not here, Toad. And I think, just for fun, I'm going to pound a few knobs on your head. With that mess of ratty hair, Mom will never see any bruises or anything."

"Shut up, Michael! I never did anything to you!"

Todd quietly finished his cereal, leaving a pool of milk at the bottom of the bowl. Michael wasn't really angry with Todd. He just enjoyed pushing his buttons and making him squirm a little... like a dog chasing a cat or a cat playing with a mouse. And because he was bigger than Todd, he assumed he could do whatever he felt like doing to his brother.

"Don't tell me to shut up, you little scum bucket," Michael shot back, and then looked up toward the ceiling with obvious satisfaction.

Rubbing his hands together, he slowly revealed his plans for this afternoon's abuse. "First, I think I'll get you in a choke hold with my left arm. Then, I'll use the knuckles of my right hand to pound the knobs on your head—like this."

Michael demonstrated by curling his left arm around an imaginary head that he brought to his chest and making pounding gestures with his right hand, as if he already had his brother in his death grip. Slowly turning around, he glared at Todd, who glared right back. With a quick flick of his wrist, Todd tossed nearly half a bowl of milk in Michael's face before bolting out of his chair.

"Augh!" Michael shrieked, jumping back a step at the unexpected assault.

Todd ran at him like a professional linebacker and hit him with a stiff arm to the chest. He shot past Michael on the left and ran out of the kitchen. He had no plan but was running in a panic.

Michael wiped the milk from his eyes and hollered after Todd, "Now you're gonna get it!" He was on his tail in an instant.

Todd ran into the dining room and around to the opposite side of the table. Now Michael really was angry. He darted right and then stopped. He jerked left and stopped again. Each time, Todd moved the opposite way.

"You know I'm faster than you, don't you?" Michael said with a devilish grin. "A lot faster."

Committed to a dead run hard to the right, Michael ran as fast as he could around the table as Todd let out an audible *augh* while running to his right. Darting for the corner behind a large potted fig tree, Todd knew that if he kept too close to the table Michael would catch him.

Michael dove low, grasping for Todd's trailing ankle but ended up on the floor with only a sock in his hand. Desperate and full of adrenalin, Todd banked off the corner wall and bolted directly toward the center of the dining room table. He didn't take the time for any dodging or faking or any change of direction. He just ran straight at the center of the table and the small gap between the chairs.

Michael looked confused until he saw Todd dive up onto the table and slide right across the top of it on his stomach, with his T-shirt and sweatpants helping him glide effortlessly across the polished wooden surface. Dropping his left arm on the table palm first, Todd pulled his knees to his chest and spun around and off the table feet first. The smooth move impressed Michael, but he was still angry about the milk in the face and wasn't about to be bested by his little brother, who was running headlong up the stairs, with Michael trailing behind.

"I've got you now!" Michael shouted. "There's nowhere for you to hide up there!"

Todd ran past his own room and headed into his brother's.

"You're dog meat, Toad!" Michael yelled.

When he reached the doorway of his room, Michael stopped dead in his tracks, staring in disbelief at Todd, who was panting and out of breath but still angry and resolute. Holding Michael's prize guitar by the neck with both hands raised high above the wooden bedpost, Todd stood like a lumberjack about to split a giant log.

"Don't... You... Dare!" Michael said, pointing a shaky finger at Todd, whose eyes widened with anticipation and then narrowed with focus and determination. "Just put the guitar on the bed and I promise I won't pound the crap out of you," he said as he moved slowly toward him, watching Todd's eyebrows narrow as he raised the guitar a little higher over the bedpost.

Michael came to a full stop. "Listen, you little dirt bag," he said through gritted teeth. "I'm gonna count to three!"

"And then what, Michael?" Todd said, cutting him off. "You're gonna watch me smash this thing into a bunch of toothpicks?"

"No. Then I'm going to smash YOU! One... two... thr—"

"Helloooo! I'm home."

Todd grinned at the sound of his mother's voice and relaxed his death grip on his brother's prize possession. "Here," he said with little emotion as he lobbed the guitar gracefully to the right side of Michael, who lunged for it with a giant step forward and to the side while Todd slid past his preoccupied brother and headed down the stairs before Michael knew what happened.

Usually, Todd would have to scream at the top of his lungs before someone would come to his rescue. It was his only other defensive strategy. Todd would scream things at Michael like, *You're hurting me!* or *Give it back!* or *You're the biggest jerk in the world!* And if Todd was lucky, his mom would be within earshot. But most of the time, Todd just tried to stay out of Michael's way by ignoring him and reading alone in his room.

Even their 13-year-old sister Jenny didn't like to get involved when it came to Michael. And she wasn't interested in protecting Todd. That was beneath her. She was totally wrapped up in her friends and social status. She liked words and had what Todd and Michael called a *word of the week.* They saw her world as a place of desperate obsession, where the goal was to stay aware and on top of everything that was *in* and *cool,* including words—especially words that could put someone in his or her place quickly and efficiently. They also called it the *word of the week* because that's about how long it took for a word to get overused and fall out of fashion with the in crowd. This week's word, or one of them, was *immature.*

On the phone with her friend Megan, Jenny was just about to learn if Eric Larson liked her or like-liked her, when Michael's teasing became too much to bear. She covered the phone with her hand and barked, "Shut up, Michael! You're so immature!"

Michael simply laughed out loud, taking it to the extreme by laughing louder and longer and coming closer and closer to Jenny, like a mad clown out of control. Pretending to be momentarily stunned by her outburst, Michael just looked at her blankly, then back at Todd, then back at her. Then, both he and Todd burst out laughing, which annoyed Jenny to no end. When she gained her composure, Jenny continued her conversation with Megan, huffing her way up the stairs, which was perfect timing because Mary Ann Preston had just come into the kitchen with the groceries. Todd's torture was over, at least for today.

"Hi, Mom," the two boys said simultaneously.

"Hi, boys. Are you behaving today?"

"Yes," Michael said.

"No," Todd replied, stepping on Michael's word and proceeding, without taking a breath, to recount some of the taunts that he had endured just minutes before.

Mary Ann put her hand up, palm facing out, and shook her head. "I don't even want to hear it," she said. "Michael, leave your brother alone. And Todd, I told you to ignore him. You know he just wants to get a reaction out of you."

Out of his mother's view, Michael nodded in agreement while making a mocking face at Todd and mouthing the words *yeah Toad*.

"Okay, okay," Todd said, indicating that he understood his mother and was willing to drop it. "He called me *Toad* again!" he haplessly blurted out in one last desperate attempt to get his brother in trouble.

"Todd, that's ENOUGH!" his mother shouted.

*Wow... that backfired,* Todd thought to himself.

"Mom?"

"Yes," Mary Ann responded, exasperated.

"When is Dad coming home?"

"Todd, you know this already. He'll be home Friday night. Late."

"Okay. I just hoped he might be home early, or that maybe you had heard something... or something."

"No. Friday night. Late."

"Okay."

"Toddy," Mary Ann said. "Help me put these groceries away and then I'll make supper."

"Alright," he replied with a smile, taking a heavy bag from her arms. Todd knew that when his mother called him *Toddy*, all was forgotten and they could start the evening anew.

The next few days went by in the same familiar way. Todd would get up, go to school, come home, get picked on by Michael, eat supper and go to bed. He actually preferred spending time in his room reading and pretending he was a character in one of the books he'd read with his father—when he was home. They'd read everything from comic books to the classics, which were Todd's favorite, especially at bedtime. For one thing, the stories were exciting and much longer than a comic book. Among his favorites were *The Adventures of Tom Sawyer*, *Moby Dick* and *20,000 Leagues Under the Sea*. He even enjoyed the newer classics, like *Cryptid Hunters* and all the Harry Potter books. The thing he liked best about stories like *Tom Sawyer* and the Harry Potter series was that they were about kids just like him, and they always came out on top in the end. They also had a sort of honor code, which he admired. These heroes would do whatever had to be done to help a friend or protect their family. Todd thought that's what made them special, and he wished he had a friend like one of them.

Though the Prestons hadn't lived in Parkerville all that long, Todd had a few friends at school, but they weren't like his storybook heroes. Because of his dad's job, Todd and his family moved more often than he liked. And none of his friends from school lived close enough so that they could just pop over to his house and play whenever they felt like it. So, for now, he would just read and imagine that he was Robin Hood, or Harry Potter, or Sir Lancelot, or Luke Skywalker.

Todd waited anxiously for Friday night, which finally came after he had dutifully gone to bed. Feeling blue because he knew his dad would be late, he was only half asleep when he heard the garage door opening, and then the sound of the back door closing. He knew his father was home.

"Dad! Dad!" Todd shouted, running down the stairs to greet him.

"Hey, buddy!" his father said as he knelt down on one knee, scooping his young son up in his arms and giving him a big hug.

"Toddy! How ya doin?" Did you miss me?"

"Yeah, I sure did!" Todd said. "Are you gonna read to me tonight?"

"Whoa, buddy. It's been a long, hard week and I'm pooped. How bout I read you two stories tomorrow night?"

"Awww," Todd said, hanging his head.

The look of complete disappointment and sadness on his son's face told Thomas Preston the whole tale.

"Alright," he finally agreed. "Let's get you up to your room so you can pick out a book."

Todd jumped onto his dad's back and held on tight around his neck and shoulders. He could smell his father's cologne as they bounded up the stairs like a horse and rider, and he felt very safe and content. He didn't understand exactly why, but to Todd, this was home.

"Well, what should we read tonight?" Thomas asked Todd. "How about *Huck Finn*?"

"No," Todd said.

"How about *King Arthur*?"

"No."

"*Ship of Dreams*? You always liked that one," Thomas reminded him.

"No," Todd replied once again.

"*Goodnight Moon*?" Thomas said with a smile.

"That's for babies!" Todd said with disdain.

"Okay, okay. What'll it be?"

"I don't know. We've pretty much read through all of these," Todd said, pointing to his library of books.

"I know!" Thomas said with delight. "How about a Sparky story?"

"What's a Sparky story?"

"Well," his father began, "Sparky was my dog when I was a boy just about your age. We did lots of things together. He would even ride on the back of my mini-bike with me."

"No way!" Todd replied with disbelief.

"Yeah, he would. He'd put his front paws on my shoulders, and off we'd go."

"Wow! Cooool!"

"So... does that mean you'd like to hear a Sparky story tonight?" he asked Todd, knowing it was the perfect time to tell him about his dog.

"Yep!" replied a very excited young boy.

# 2

"Okay... where should I start?" Thomas said under his breath. "I guess I'll start just a little before the beginning—"

"How can you do that?" Todd interrupted.

"Just listen," his father replied. "You know how your Grandpa Rich is pretty smart and a good carpenter?"

"Yeah."

"Alright, well, one day I came home from my friend's house and Grandpa Rich was down in the basement building a big wooden box. The outside was plywood with a pine frame around each side. And all the insides and the bottom of the box were covered with carpet."

"What was the box for?" Todd asked.

"That's the funny part," Thomas replied. "I asked your grandpa the same thing, and he told me it was a box for school books. I really thought he was just going to set it somewhere and store books in it."

"What about the carpet?" Todd asked.

"That's what I asked Grandpa Rich, too! He said, 'Oh, that's so the books don't slide around and get wrecked when I'm driving back and forth to school with them in the trunk of my car.' Now, I was only about 10 years old, but I thought your grandpa had lost his mind. In the first place, HE was the teacher. It's not like he needed his books for homework. In the second place, I'd never seen him bring home more than one or two books before. In the third place, there was no way on God's green earth that this big wooden box was ever going to fit in the trunk of his car! I mean, even I could see that his explanation didn't make sense."

"So, what was it really for, Dad?" asked Todd.

"It was for Sparky... his dog house," said Thomas. "He had to tell me that story so it wouldn't spoil the surprise that he already got a dog for the family."

Todd chuckled a little and said, "That's pretty cool."

"Yes, the diversion worked, and I quickly forgot all about the big wooden box with the carpet inside."

"So, when did you get Sparky?" asked Todd.

"I got him on Christmas Day. We had just finished opening all our presents and everyone was in a cheerful mood. The smell of the blue spruce tree and freshly baked Christmas cookies filled the house, and your grandpa had this little glimmer in his eye and a grin on this face, like he was up to something. Suddenly, Grandpa Rich got up from his chair, looked right at me and, with that grin, told me to put my slippers on because he needed my help in the garage."

"Were you still in your pajamas?" Todd asked.

"Yep," Thomas replied. "And it was a pretty cold day, too. But I was so curious that I did what Grandpa Rich asked me to do and hopped right into my slippers and followed him out to the garage. Grandpa had this old VW van that he used as a carpenter's truck for his building projects outside of school. He told me he needed something out of the van, but I knew he was up to something. Your grandpa's surprises were usually pretty good, so I was expecting something great."

"What did you find?" Todd asked excitedly.

"Nothing—at first."

Todd looked confused. "Nothing?" he asked with disappointment.

"Well, when I pulled open the side door of the van, all I saw was about six bags of concrete mix on the floor. So, I pulled my head out of the van and... I'm sure I looked pretty confused... I told Grandpa Rich that all I could see was cement, so he told me to look a little harder. 'There is something else in there,' he said. So, I put my head back in and looked all the way to the back ledge that covered the engine compartment. I could just make out the silhouette of a small black dog sitting in the dark on the back bench. I yelled from inside the van, *IT'S A DOG!* And I could hear Grandpa Rich laugh as I made my way to the back."

"What was the dog doing?" Todd asked.

"The dog was just sitting there in the dark and hadn't made a sound—"

"Were you afraid?" Todd interrupted again.

"I remember being a little cautious," Thomas admitted. "But, as I made my way closer and over the cement bags to get a dog that I hadn't met yet in the back of a dark van, my eyes became more accustom to the dark, and I could see his tail wag and slap the cushion of the back seat with a bap, bap, bap, which would become a very familiar sound."

"Did Grandpa Rich give him the name Sparky?" Todd asked.

"No. Grandpa Rich thought that I should name him."

"Wow!" Todd shouted.

"Yeah, I thought that was pretty great, too, even though I had never named anything before. After a few minutes, your grandma and my sisters were on the scene. They were petting the dog and offering suggestions for names, of course. Grandma Karen had a look of pure joy on her face. Then, Grandpa Rich knelt down beside me on one knee and said, 'Ya know, when I was about your age I had a dog, too, and his name was Sparky.' Grandma smiled even wider."

"And you thought that was a good name for a dog, too... right, Dad?"

"I sure did!" Thomas exclaimed. "And Grandma Karen knew Grandpa Rich really wanted that name. I had heard of names like Rover, and Rex, and Spot, and Fido, but I hadn't heard of Sparky before. Come to find out, that was because I was only 10 years old. Sparky was actually a pretty popular name for a dog back then."

"Did Sparky get to sleep in your bed that night?" Todd asked hopefully.

"Well, I asked Grandpa Rich that very question and he said maybe not in my bed, but he could sleep on my sleeping bag if I wanted to sleep in it on the floor."

"So, is that what you did, Dad?"

"Yep. Sparky slept with me on the sleeping bag for the next few nights. That gave Grandpa Rich enough time to put the roof on the dog house and make room for it in the corner of the garage. Of course, I got to help with this little project. And when the roof was finally intact, I suddenly remembered the story about it being a box for his school books. I looked at my dad, pointed my finger right at his face and told him I knew it wasn't for books. There was no way that would fit in the trunk of his car!"

"What did Grandpa Rich say?"

"He just laughed and said, 'You knew it, huh? Well, I'm glad you stopped asking me questions that night cuz I didn't want you to find out what it was really for. It's a pretty good dog house though, don't ya think?' I sure did think so. Carpeted wall to wall and ceiling to floor for comfort and insulation."

Thomas paused. "Hum," he said reflectively, "I can still smell the fresh cut lumber from helping with the dog house... silly, huh?"

"I don't smell anything," Todd said.

Thomas smiled and said, "No, I'm sure you don't, now go to sleep.

*******

20

The next morning was Saturday. Todd came down to breakfast rubbing his eyes. "What're we havin?" he asked his mom through a yawn.

"Oh, honey, just have some toaster waffles. I have to run," she said, heading for the back door with her planner under one arm and her oversized purse in the other. "I have a volunteer meeting for the Park Planning Committee, and then a function at the Art Center. Not sure when I'll be home. Bye!"

Todd didn't like the fact that his mom was so busy. Saturday was one of the few days he could do things with her. But it seemed that hadn't happened for a long time. Despite his disappointment, he made his waffles, remembering to turn down the toaster to a lower setting than his mother liked. He was quite proud when they came out with just the perfect tint of gold, barely detectable to any adult.

Todd had nearly finished his breakfast by the time Michael walked in with his bathrobe open and his pajama bottoms pulled way up over his navel. Todd couldn't help but smile.

"There's the smart feller... or is it the other way around?" Michael joked, giving Todd a little swat on the brim of his baseball cap before pouring himself a bowl of cereal and sitting next to Todd at the breakfast table without incident.

Seconds later, Jenny wandered into the kitchen, still not quite awake. When she saw the two boys sitting quietly together, she stopped in her tracks. "What's wrong with you two?" she said with mild shock.

Thomas came in right behind her and went straight to the fridge for some orange juice.

"What are we gonna do today, Dad?" Todd inquired eagerly.

"Well, we are going to let me have some breakfast, and then we are going to let me take a shower, and then we are going to clean our rooms, and do our chores. And when I say *we*, I mean *you*."

"Awww," a collective groan erupted from the Preston children.

"Come on now... a little hard work never hurt anyone," Thomas replied.

"Awww," came the response from the family again.

"Besides, you know Saturday is chore day. So, we are going to clean our rooms, and we are going to sweep out the garage, and we are going to make lunch for your mom and do the dishes. And again, when I say *we*, I mean *you*."

"I don't think Mom will be home for lunch, Dad," Todd said.

"Why? Where is she?"

"Some town park thing and some art thing."

"Oh." Thomas seemed surprised. "Did she say when she'd be back?"

"She said she didn't know. But can we go bowling after our chores are done?"

"Oh... not today, buddy. I have a presentation for work that's due on Monday."

"Awww," came the response from the whole family again.

"Dad, you're never here!" Jenny whined.

"Hey, I'm just trying to get ahead in life, ya know," he said defensively. "And a little hard work never hurt anyone. That's what my dad used to say. And I need to go the extra mile right now so that Mom and I can keep a roof over this family's head... and send you guys to some good schools down the road."

"But it's been forever since we've done anything fun together," Jenny said dramatically. "I can't remember when I've been so distraught!"

Todd and Michael looked slyly at each other and simultaneously whispered, "Word of the week."

"Shut up, you big delinquents!" Jenny yelled.

"Ooooh," Michael said mockingly, then looked at Todd with a quizzical expression. "Word of the month?"

"Alright, alright, that's enough!" Thomas said firmly. "I'm sorry, but I really have to get this presentation ready for work. So, you guys do your chores and I'll try and finish my work, and we'll do something fun tomorrow."

"You promise?" Todd asked.

"I promise."

With that, the Preston children began dutifully doing their chores well into the afternoon, making their beds, sweeping the floors, and cleaning their bedrooms. And when Mary Ann called to say she'd be late, Jenny even stepped up, preparing a fine meal of chicken and rice, green beans, and a lettuce salad, which they all enjoyed for dinner. And after a quick run around the kitchen, with everyone helping to clean up, Michael, Todd and Jenny were allowed to watch TV, which would finally allow their parents to enjoy some peace and quiet.

"How is that presentation coming along," Mary Ann asked Thomas.

"Honestly, it could be better," he admitted. "It's not quite where I want it to be yet."

"We're still gonna do something fun tomorrow though, aren't we, Dad?" asked Todd, who was listening and thought his parents had a weird way of saying things, like wanting a presentation to be somewhere else, as if his dad could drive it around and park it somewhere.

"Ah... yeah, sure we will," Thomas hesitantly told his youngest son.

After an hour of TV, it was time for Todd to go to bed, and time for Thomas to read to him.

"What should we read tonight, buddy?"

"Can you tell me some more about Sparky?" Todd asked excitedly.

"Sure, I can! What would you like to know?"

"I don't know... did he do any tricks?" Todd asked hopefully.

"Well, sure, Sparky could do some tricks," Thomas replied. "But not right away. I had to teach him what I wanted him to do. Sparky was only about a year old when we got him and he came from a shelter, so he didn't really know any tricks. And we didn't know for sure how old he was right away. Grandpa Rich had to take him to the veterinarian to get some shots before he could come home with us. It was the doctor who thought Sparky must be about a year old."

"What did he look like?"

"I was just about to tell you," Thomas replied. "We were told Sparky was a Beagle-Terrier mix. He was a little bigger than a Beagle and had floppy ears like a Beagle, but he was all black and white. There was no brown, like you see on most Beagles. His face looked like a Beagle's, too, or a small black Lab. But you know what was really cool? It was *where* he was black and white."

"What d'ya mean, Dad?"

"I mean, he was mostly a black dog with short, shiny black hair, but he had four white paws and a white tip at the end of his tail. And that's not all that was unusual. He also had a white tummy and a white triangle on the back of his neck. It started out wide at the base of his neck, just about where his collar was and then came up to a point just below the back of his head. And I'll tell you what... if you would have cut that white triangle from a piece of cloth and laid it down on the back of that dog's neck, you couldn't have put it any more in the middle than where that white mark was on my dog!"

"Huh, ha," Todd giggled slightly.

"That's not all," Thomas continued. "He had a white stripe that started on his forehead, just above his eyebrows, and worked its way down his face between his eyes."

Todd giggled again. "A dog with eyebrows," he said through a laugh.

"Dogs have eyebrows," Thomas said firmly. "Anyway, the white stripe started there and came straight down the center of his face about as wide as a pencil. When it came to his nose, it spread out and draped over both sides of his muzzle."

"What's a muzzle?" Todd asked.

"It's sort of the top and sides of a dog's nose—the furry part but not the tip of his nose," he explained. "The tip of Sparky's nose was black. I told you his tummy was white, right?"

"Yeah."

"Well, basically, his whole underside was white from under his chin and down his throat to his chest and all the way to his hind legs."

"What about his tricks?" Todd asked, reminding his dad to get to the point. "What could he do?"

"Well, this wasn't actually a trick," Thomas began, "but you need to know this part before I tell you why I thought he could do his best trick ever."

Now Todd could hardly wait to hear about this great trick.

"When I would come home from school, or when I would take him out to play, Sparky would run and jump at my chest. It was like he wanted me to hold him when we first saw each other. He would jump and jump, but I was too small to catch him. So, I took his front paws in my hands and told him to jump. And then, using his hind legs and pressing down with his front paws, he would jump! And right into my arms he would come."

"Cool!"

"This got to be a pretty regular thing. I would hold him and pet him for a little while, and then I'd put him down and he wouldn't jump at my chest anymore."

"So, what was the trick?" Todd asked again.

"Alright, this is the second thing you need to know before I tell you about the trick."

"Awww!" Todd said impatiently.

"Grandpa Rich had a friend a long time ago named Roy Watkins. He would tell me stories about Roy's dog Petey, who would ride on the back of his bike. Roy had some kind of carrier box over the back fender and his dog would stand in it, put his paws on Roy's shoulders, and off they'd go."

"What a cool trick!"

"Let me tell you, I thought that was the coolest trick I'd ever heard of."

"Did you teach Sparky to ride on your bike, Dad?"

"Well, I couldn't because my bike didn't have anything but a skinny fender over the back wheel."

"So, what did you do?"

"First, I wanted to see if I could get Sparky on my back. You know how I told you he would jump into my arms if I helped him with his front paws? Well, I brought him into the back yard on the grass so that if it didn't work, he could just jump down. Then, I took his front paws into my hands, like we had done a hundred times before. Only this time, I crossed my hands in front of me—like this." Thomas stood beside the bed to show Todd what he meant and used Todd's stuffed bear Benjamin to demonstrate.

"This time, when I said *up* to Sparky and he jumped, I pulled and spun under him. So, instead of bringing him to my chest, I brought one paw to each of my shoulders." Thomas demonstrated again with the stuffed bear.

"Next, I just leaned forward a little and let go with my left hand, putting it across the back of my belt so I could catch his hind legs with my left forearm and hold on to one front paw with my right hand, and it worked on the very first try!" he exclaimed. "There we stood for about thirty seconds. Sparky didn't even try to jump down. And I had a good hold of him, too! Finally, it was time for me to find out if Sparky was afraid of my mini-bike."

"You got a mini-bike for Christmas, too!"

"No, that was about four years later. And I paid for half of that mini-bike myself, I'll have you know. Anyway, I brought Sparky to the mini-bike and started it up. Then, I hopped on the seat and revved it up a few times."

"Was Sparky afraid?"

"Not at all!" Todd's dad replied. "He just grabbed my pant leg, like he didn't want me to go. You see, Sparky was an outdoor dog, and when he got the chance to be out of his kennel, he loved it. I'm sure he just didn't want me to leave."

Thomas continued, enjoying the story as much as Todd. "With the motor idling, I brought Sparky closer to the mini-bike. I leaned over one side and crossed my arms in front of me. I took hold of Sparky's front paws, and when I said *up*, he jumped. I spun under him and he landed with his front paws right on my shoulders. His back feet landed right on the seat of the mini bike and the side of his face was over my left shoulder and right next to my face. I put my right hand on the handlebars, patted him reassuringly with my left, and I started to move the mini-bike with my feet, you know, like a scooter. And Sparky stayed right there! When it was time to give it some gas, I slowly turned the throttle and *burrr-rup-bup-baaaah*, went the mini-bike."

"That's awesome, Dad!" Todd said, grinning.

"Sparky and I made a full loop around the back yard. He really seemed to like it. And from that day on, the two of us rode together a lot. But I knew I had to show my dad. So, when Grandpa Rich got home, I told him I had something to show him. He said, 'Alright, let's see it.' So, I got Sparky on that mini-bike and made the loop around the yard one more time, and then drove back to my dad. He had the biggest smile on his face and just watched us, shaking his head. 'Well, I'll be!' was all he said. But he was all smiles."

"Where did you and Sparky go on your mini-bike?" Todd asked.

"I'd ride with my friends in a field just down the road from home and along the local roads," Thomas told him. "We would ride down State Aid Road Number Four to the old Township Hall on the corner, then to the right along old St. Joe Road, which passed in front of Westwood School. I remember riding piggyback style with Sparky so often that I didn't give much thought to what a cool trick it was anymore. Then, one day we were riding in the field across from the school and a car full of kids was driving on the road alongside of us. I glanced over and saw a girl frantically tapping the driver on the shoulder, pointing in our direction."

"They must of thought you were pretty cool," Todd said.

Thomas smiled. "That's when I remember thinking yep, that's about the coolest trick I'd ever heard of."

"Wow, that's a great story, Dad. Did it really happen?"

"It sure did, buddy... just like that... and Sparky really loved it."

Todd nodded. "Yeah, that must have been pretty good."

"Okay, time for bed," Thomas said abruptly.

"Awww," Todd protested.

"I'll tell you another story tomorrow," Thomas reassured him as he pulled up the covers and tucked them in around Todd. "Night, buddy," he said, turning out the light.

"Night, Dad," came Todd's sleepy voice out of the darkened room.

## 3

"Time for church," Mrs. Preston announced, moving from one room to the next in an attempt to roust everyone from bed. She smiled while she listened to the usual minor grumblings, knowing that what was causing the stir was just the idea of having an obligation on a Sunday morning after a busy week rather than the idea of going to church itself. And though week after week it was the same routine, the Preston family always managed to have a nice breakfast and still promptly arrive for service, with plans for something fun in the afternoon.

"Okay, last week Jenny got to decide the activity, so it's *my* turn this time," said Todd.

"Can we go bowling or to the go-kart track?" he asked excitedly.

"Eew!" Jenny responded instantly. "No way! How juvenile!"

"Oh yeah? Well guess what, Jenny? We ARE juveniles!" Todd shouted.

Michael was listening to one of his favorite bands on his headphones, uncharacteristically out of the conversation.

The argument continued like this for another minute or two, with Michael dancing in and out of the immediate area between Todd and Jenny while listening to music only he could hear.

"That's ENOUGH!" Thomas shouted.

Everyone stopped, as if someone yelled *freeze*, except for Michael, who was still dancing around and enjoying the fact that he was annoying his brother and sister. When he noticed that no one was moving or talking anymore, he finally stopped and pulled out one side of his headphones so that he could hear what was happening.

"I know all of you were looking forward to doing something fun today," Thomas started.

Todd's heart sank. *Were?* he thought to himself. *This isn't going to be good.*

"But, I'm sorry to have to tell you... I still have to finish my presentation for tomorrow, and I'm not sure how long that's going to take."

The look of disappointment on everyone's face was extreme and hard for Thomas to handle, but he felt it was his only choice. He wanted his work to stand out, and he knew that with a little more time, it would.

"I'll tell you what," Thomas said. "I'll get going on my presentation, and tonight we'll watch a movie."

"Tonight?" Michael whined. "What about today?"

"Yeah, Dad. You promised," moaned Jenny.

Todd just hung his head and moved slowly away from his family toward the bottom of the stairs, where he began the long climb to his bedroom. He knew, with his father's mind made up, he may as well find some other way to entertain himself.

Michael and Jenny were still desperately trying to reverse their father's decision, but all the cajoling fell on deaf ears. Even Mary Ann voiced her disappointment with her husband's position, since he had promised them some family fun the day before.

"You really can be a jerk sometimes, you know that?" she scolded him with a clear look of disgust on her face before heading up the stairs to see if she could console her youngest son.

"Toddy," she called, arriving at the top of the stairs. "Where are you?"

Todd was face down, crossways on his bed, with his head hanging so far over the back side that at first glance he appeared headless.

"Toddy," Mary Ann said softly, sitting on his bed and rubbing his back.

Todd rolled over with tear-filled eyes and said, "He promised!"

"I know, honey, but this presentation is very important to your father."

Todd's eyebrows narrowed. "More important than us?"

"No, honey," she reassured him. "But I'm not going to make excuses for him either. I'll tell you what... let's you and I do something fun. Just the two of us."

"What about Michael and Jenny?" Todd asked.

"I'll talk to them. I'm sure Michael can find something to do with his friend, Kurt. And I'll drop off Jenny at Megan's. Then you and I will go and have some fun."

Todd's face brightened just a little, and Mary Ann knew she was on the right track.

*******

That afternoon, once the older kids were with their friends, Todd and his mother made their way to the mall. They started out with some ice cream for Todd and some window shopping for Mary Ann before heading down the street to a local sporting goods store called Rossco's. It had everything from soccer balls and hunting knives to fishing boats and *The Rock Wall*, which was located next to a large center staircase. It had an obstacle course for climbers to test the gear they were thinking of buying. On the weekends, someone was on hand to provide instruction, as well as belay the rope for climbers trying to make their way to the top.

Todd turned on his heels toward his mother with a huge smile. "Can I?" he asked.

"Sure," Mary Ann said without hesitation. "Let's get you geared up."

Todd donned a helmet and a harness. After some brief instruction, he was on his way up the rock wall. He went up and down several times and was actually quite good for his age. When he finished, the belayer gave him a high five and said, "Nice job!" This put a big, proud smile on Todd's face. Mary Ann smiled, too. Feeling his pleasure was the best part of her day.

Their next stop was the art museum, where Mary Ann planned to drop off some papers and speak with her friend, Reggie, about the upcoming art show. He was not only well educated in art but was also a handsome man in his early forties, with dark wavy hair. He had the considerable gift of being able to converse with anyone on a wide range of topics.

"Have a look around, Todd," Mary Ann said. "We'll head home in a minute."

Todd knew his mother would be more than a minute, so he decided to check out the museum, which wasn't open to the public on Sunday. Reggie switched on some lights to let Todd explore.

Leaving the office area, he turned right and walked straight to the well-lit glass showcase filled with Bill Baird's marionettes, some of which had been made for *The Sound of Music* and other children's television shows of the fifties and sixties. Todd had recently seen *The Sound of Music* with his mom. It was one of her favorite movies, and they had watched it together when he was home sick a month ago. He recognized that several of the puppets in the showcase were from the movie and thought they were pretty cool. Some were not as familiar, like the big birds with bright feathers and cartoon-like faces. Their long stork-like legs were made from lightweight rope and had brightly painted wooden beads for the knee and elbow joints and big, yellow wooden feet. Todd smiled and thought about how fun it would be to make them—and play with them. Yet, he noticed how different the puppets looked from the movie without any movement at all. He felt a little sad to see them just hanging alone and still, and no one playing with them. In a small corner at one end of the showcase, he noticed a small, black and white cat with four white paws and its tail tipped in white. It made him think of Sparky and his father's stories, and what he must have been like as a boy. He thought about how his father's face lit up when he was telling Todd about his dog. He hadn't seen his father that happy in a long time, and he liked it. He wondered if his father was happy now. And if he was, why he didn't seem to show it.

Todd turned to look at the cat one more time, but it now had long floppy ears and a long nose—like a dog. He blinked his eyes and looked again, only to see the cat looking like a cat. He felt a sudden chill, with the hair on his forearms and the back of his neck standing up. "Wow," he said quietly, thinking that was weird. "Hmm... still a cat."

"Come on, Toddy," Mary Ann called. "It's time to go."

The sound of his mother's voice drew Todd's attention away from the cat. *Wow, it must have just been my imagination,* he thought, then quickly replied, "Coming, Mom!"

Todd walked slowly beside his mother. When they reached the front entrance, he stopped and turned to her. "It's okay, you know," he stated without finishing his sentence.

"What's okay?" Mary Ann asked.

"It's okay that you brought me here."

"Well, why wouldn't it be okay?" Mary asked, a little confused.

"Because you said this was going to be a day just for you and me," Todd reminded her. "Then, you stopped here to take care of business with Reggie, and I just wanted you to know that it's okay."

Mary Ann looked at Todd with a slight frown, still not quite sure what he meant. Todd could tell she didn't understand. "It's just that you got really upset with Dad when he broke his promise about doing something fun today with the family. So, I just want you to know it's okay. I know grown-ups have to do some things they don't always want to do sometimes."

Mary Ann looked at him for a long time and replayed his words over and over in her mind on the way home. She presumed that, in his mind, she had done exactly the same thing to him that Thomas had done to the family by putting work ahead of them on a family day—Sunday.

The drive home was quiet. Mary Ann kept glancing at Todd to see if she could tell, for sure, if things were really okay. When they pulled into the driveway and parked the car, Todd got out and said, "Thanks, Mom. That was fun."

"You always say thank you," she said with a smile, thinking that was the second-best part of her day.

The rest of the evening went by quickly, and when bedtime approached, Todd washed his face, brushed his teeth and climbed under his covers.

It wasn't long before Thomas entered his room. "Did you say your prayers, buddy?" he asked Todd, who nodded.

"Listen, I'm sorry we didn't do something fun today," he said apologetically.

"That's okay," Todd replied.

"I really needed to get that presentation just right."

"Are you happy, Dad?" Todd asked his father with an inquisitive look.

"What? Am I happy?" Thomas repeated Todd's question. "Ah, yeah, ah sure, I'm happy... I guess. Why?"

"I just wondered." Todd replied.

Thomas looked pensively at Todd and thought... *what an odd question.* Then, he sort of snapped out of it and asked, "What would you like to read tonight, Todd?"

"Tell me some more about Sparky!"

"You want to hear some more about Sparky, eh?" Thomas replied with a smile. "Well, I told you he was an outside dog, right?"

"Yep."

"Well, one thing I remember about Sparky was that when it was cold, Grandma Karen would let him come in the house to sleep with me. My bedroom was in the basement, and Sparky would have to walk from the garage into the house, through the family room and the dining room to the stairway door and then go down the steps to my room. When I would let him into the house from the garage, he would first stay on the rug by the doorway. Then, with his head hanging down a little bit, he'd look to see if any grown-ups were nearby. Usually, I would already have the door to the stairway open so that if the coast was clear, he only had about a 15-foot straight shot from the back-door rug to the stairway, then to freedom... and a warm night in a bed with his boy."

"Ha, ha... you?" Todd said.

"Yes, me," Thomas replied. "The funniest thing was that he would not move from the rug until he thought it was absolutely safe. He would get down low to the floor, like he was crawling through some invisible tunnel. But, he was just trying to make himself as small and inconspicuous as possible."

"Why?" Todd asked.

"So that no one would see him and put him back out in the garage! Sparky would slowly put one foot in front of the other, his tummy almost on the floor, and as he got closer and closer to the stair door, he would move faster and faster until he hit the top of the steps. Then, he would go down so fast, like he was on a slide—shooom! His little feet were just a blur, but his head and body appeared frozen as he flew down those stairs. And when he got to the bottom of the steps, he would stop and turn around and wait for me with his tail wagging hard, head cocked to one side and very happy that he had made it."

"That's funny," Todd said. "What else do you remember?"

"Well, Grandpa Rich had a small aluminum fishing boat that he allowed me to take out when we finished working on the cabin for the day. Sparky and I would hop in that boat and go for a ride, or maybe fish for a little bit."

"Sparky sure liked being with you, didn't he, Dad!"

"He sure did! And what I liked most about having Sparky in the boat was that he would stand right up front with his hind paws on the boat floor and his front paws on the point of the bow while we were moving! His ears would float in the wind, almost straight out from his head. He looked like maybe he could fly!"

"Ha! That's funny," Todd chuckled. "Do you miss him, Dad?"

"Yeah, I guess so," he said, looking a little sad and realizing that before he started telling Todd about his dog, he hadn't really thought about him in a long time. "He sure was a good dog."

"Do you think Grandpa Rich misses him?" Todd asked.

"Ya know, I don't know," he replied. "But one thing I do know is that your Grandpa Rich is an old softy. And I'll bet if you ask him about Sparky, you'll get a great big smile. And maybe even another story or two about that little dog. But right now, it's time for bed, mister."

Todd smiled. As he rolled over, Thomas gently pulled the covers up and over his shoulders. It was the perfect end to his special day.

# 4

Early the next morning, Thomas was in the driveway loading Grandpa Rich's van with everything he needed for his big presentation. Rich helped Thomas load the luggage, then they grabbed their travel coffee mugs and climbed into the van. The two men traveled in silence for several minutes. Thomas had notes to review and was checking his itinerary. When he finally looked up, he caught his father staring at him. "What?" Thomas asked.

His dad smiled. "Oh, nothing."

Thomas gave him a look, as if peering over the top of some half-moon reading glasses. "Don't give me that!" he said. "What's on your mind?"

"Well, to tell you the truth, I was just wondering something," Rich said.

"What?" Thomas asked.

"I was just wondering if you're happy?"

"What? Yeah... of course I'm happy... what kind of question is that? Have you been talking to Todd?"

"What? No! I haven't said anything to Todd. Why?"

"Well, because he asked me the same thing just last night!"

"No," Rich reassured him. "I've just been noticing a few things lately, and it sort of makes me wonder if... I... um—" Rich paused while he tried to find the right words. "I wonder if I could have been a better father to you and your sisters?"

"What?! What the heck are you talking about?"

"Well, Thomas, as parents we always try to do right by our kids. Teach them right from wrong. Make sure they can take care of themselves. Help them find their way in the world, ya know."

"And what? You think I've lost my way or something?"

"Thomas, all I want for you in this world is to be happy. To find some sense of purpose, something that you can be passionate about. To find your dream and go after it—that, and to raise a good family that will do the same."

"Geez, Dad! Are you kidding me with this right now? I'm getting ready to give the biggest presentation of my career this afternoon, and you bring this up? NOW? Where on earth is this coming from anyway?"

"Thomas, you're a good person and a good man, but it seems to me that you've got some of your priorities mixed up. You spend all your time chasing some idea of success, or position, or money, and you don't see anything else. I never hear you talk about your work with any passion. You're always gone. You hardly ever see your kids, and you work late all the time. When was the last time you took a family vacation? In three or four years, Michael will be out of the house. That time goes by fast, and you can't get it back!"

"Look Dad, there's nothing wrong with hard work. You taught me that. I'm just trying to get ahead, ya know?" Thomas said defensively. "And you're the one who taught me that a man's got to provide for his family."

"Yes, I did. But at what cost?" his father asked. "You're a successful man and I'm proud of you. But, I think you've got some far-off goal not even YOU know what it is. Can you tell me what it is, or how much is enough?"

"What are you saying? That money is the root of all evil and now I'm a bad person or something?"

"No, Thomas. Money is not the root of all evil. Selfishness is."

"So now you're saying I'm selfish, Dad?"

"No. I'm simply correcting you, which is part of my job as a parent," Rich continued. "Many people get it wrong and think it's about money, but it's selfishness that's the root of all evil," he said again.

"Awww, come on, Dad," Thomas replied. "I don't want to talk about this now. I've got one of the most important meetings of my career coming up in a few hours and I don't need this right now!"

"Look, son," Rich said, "I don't mean to upset you, but tell me two things—honestly. First, are you passionate about your work, or is this just the best way you've found to get a paycheck? Second, how will you know when you're a success?"

Thomas was clearly becoming irritated. "Dad, I STILL don't know where this is coming from," he answered incredulously. "Do you expect me to have an answer for you just like THAT?"

"Thomas, please think about it. That's all I ask. Now, I won't bug you about it anymore, okay?"

Rich fell silent. The confrontation was over as quickly as it had started, and they sat quietly the rest of the drive. When they reached the airport, Rich helped Thomas unload everything from the van for his flight. When it was time to leave, Thomas reached out to shake his father's hand.

"Thanks for the early morning help, Dad," he said.

Rich grabbed his son's hand and pulled him close and hugged him. "I love you, buddy," he said as he patted Thomas warmly on the back.

"I love you, too, Dad," Thomas said sincerely, though he wasn't quite sure what to make of this whole thing.

"Be safe," Rich said as Thomas turned to leave. "And think about what I said."

Thomas turned toward him with a slight smile and nodded, giving his dad that same look he'd given him in the car, as if to say mockingly, "Yessss, Dad."

Thomas boarded the plane and Rich started for home. During the long flight to Houston, he couldn't help but think about what his father had said. He tried to concentrate on his notes for his presentation, but those two questions popped into his head again and again: *What does he mean, passionate about my work? It's work! Who likes their work all the time?* Thomas thought to himself. *How will I know when I'm successful? I'll know,* he thought, *I just need a little more time. Am I happy? What? Don't I seem happy? I'm happy enough.* He continued fighting with himself. *This is foolish! I have a good job, and I need to get some things done!*

That same afternoon, Todd heard a knock at the front door of the Preston home. He peeked out the front window and ran to the door. "Grandma! Grandpa!" he yelled as he threw the front door open. "Hi! What are you doing here?"

"Oh, I was talking to your Grandma Karen about taking your dad to the airport this morning, and we both thought it would be a good idea to come visit our favorite grandson."

"It IS a good idea!" Todd said, ushering in his grandparents and closing the door behind them.

"What have you been up to, Todd?" Grandma Karen asked.

"Oh, school mostly, but Mom took me rock climbing this weekend at Rossco's sporting goods store by the mall."

"Oh, my! That sounds pretty dangerous," said Grandma Karen.

"Naw, they have ya all strapped into a harness and stuff," Todd explained.

"Well, I'm glad because I wouldn't want anything to happen to you,"

Grandma Karen said.

"No, I'm fine," replied Todd.

"Hey, Grandpa, do you remember Sparky?"

"Your dad's dog from when he was a boy? I sure do!" he said smiling. "Why do you ask?"

"Because Dad's been telling me about him at night before I go to bed."

"Ah... that's a fine thing," Rich said. "Did he tell you about the time we were working on the cabin and Sparky got into it with a skunk?"

"N-no ho, ho!" Todd said through a laugh.

"Well, we were building our second cabin out on Horseshoe Lake, ya know. It was mid-summer, so it stayed light out til... oh, 9 or 9:30 at night. So, it must have been about 10 because we had just gone to bed in the back of an old pickup I had with a topper on the back. Your dad and I were in the back of that truck in our sleeping bags on these old chaise lounge chairs, you know, like your mom sunbathes on. Sparky was in back there with us, and he starts scratching and sniffing at the tailgate and whimpering to get out. I figure he's just got to go potty, so I let him out."

"Weren't you worried about him?" Todd asked.

"No, not really, because there really wasn't anyone around he could bother," said Grandpa Rich. "So, he's out of the truck about five minutes and starts barking. Not just a barking-at-the-moon bark, or a *hey, is there anyone out here?* type bark, but a real sort of *I gotta protect my family* kind of bark. Your dad and I figured that something was up, so we opened the back end of that topper nice and slow, and there was Sparky about 40 yards away, right under the only streetlight for about a half mile, nose to nose with a skunk!"

"Woah! What did you do, Grandpa?"

"Well... I'll tell you what, Todd. We hopped outta that truck in our undershorts yelling for that dog and yelling at that skunk, trying to find a rock to throw and scare that skunk away. Finally, the skunk went down into the weeds in the ditch, and Sparky came back to us waggin' his tail, all proud of himself that he'd chased that skunk away. And did he stink!"

Todd was giggling now and holding his stomach. He kept on giggling as Grandpa Rich finished the story.

"We figured that Sparky was lucky because even though he stunk, I had smelled a skunk spray before and I was sure that he hadn't taken a direct hit. But, I was also sure that dog wasn't sleeping with us inside the back of that pickup truck! We didn't have a leash or rope with us, so we got the only thing we could find to tie him up with, which was a big electrical extension cord from our work on the cabin."

"How did you get rid of the smell?" Todd asked.

"The next day, your dad took him down to the lake and got him good and wet, then scrubbed him down with a bar of soap and got him good and wet again to rinse the soap away."

"Did that take care of the smell?" Todd asked.

"Pretty much," Grandpa Rich said. "I knew then that we were all lucky because a direct hit would have taken a lot more washing to get rid of."

"That's a funny story, Grandpa," Todd said, still laughing a little.

Grandma Karen was smiling. She'd heard the tale before but really enjoyed how much Todd liked hearing it.

"Um, Grandpa?" Todd asked.

"Yeah, buddy?"

"Was Dad a good builder like you?"

"Well, not at first. Nobody starts out being a good builder. There's too much to learn," he said. "But he learned fast, and he was always a good helper."

Todd smiled and said, "I'd like to build something someday."

"What would you like to build?" asked Grandpa Rich.

"Oh, I don't know... a tree house maybe, or a dog house for a dog of my own," replied Todd.

"I remember something about Sparky, Todd," Grandma Karen chimed in. "Would you like to hear it?"

"Sure, Grandma!" Todd replied with wide eyes.

"One day, we had taken your dad and Sparky up to see your dad's uncle, Doug. He had a cabin up near Grand Rapids, Minnesota. Grandpa Rich, your dad and Uncle Doug had gone off to a special, super-secret fishing spot that only Uncle Doug knew about."

"Did they bring Sparky?" Todd asked.

"No," said Grandma Karen. "Little Sparky had to stay at the cabin with me and Doug's wife Clarice because, as Uncle Doug said, 'A little john boat full of flyin' treble hooks is no darn place for a dog!' Well, anyway, those boys had been gone fishing for a little over an hour, and Clarice and I were talking and playing cards by the kitchen window when I saw Sparky do the darndest thing."

"What? What did he do, Grandma?" Todd asked excitedly.

"Well, I'll tell you what. That little dog came trotting up the hill towards the cabin with a stick in his mouth. Then, he turned around and sat down and dropped the stick on the ground by his front paws and looked around for a few seconds. After that, he bent down, tucked his nose under that stick and flipped it down the hill. With a quick lift of his head, he ran down the hill and pranced and pawed at that stick. Then he picked it up and came trotting back up the hill with that stick in his mouth and started all over again. That darn dog was playing fetch with himself! Can you believe that?" Grandma Karen said laughing.

Todd shook his head and smiled.

Grandma Karen said, "I never heard of such a thing. Not before nor since. I guess he just got bored waiting for his master to come home, so he found a way to entertain himself."

Todd spoke through a big smile now and said, "I wish I could have known Sparky."

Karen smiled big, too. "Yes. I wish you could have known Sparky, too. Your dad sure loved that dog."

# 5

The door from the garage to the kitchen burst open and in came Jenny and Michael, who was about to make another nasty comment to her when he heard Grandpa Rich say in his booming voice, "There they are!"

In mid-sentence, with his finger still pointed at Jenny's face, Michael turned as he said, "Oh, ah... hi, Grandpa."

Jenny ran to Grandma Karen and began to tell her all about school, her friend Megan, the awesome shoes she had seen at Carlson's in the mall, this cute guy named Eric Larson, and on and on.

Mary Ann followed through the back door a short time later with groceries under each arm. "Hi, Karen. Hi, Rich," she said. "Wanna stay for supper?"

"Oh no, hun," replied Rich. "We just wanted a short visit and then we'll get out of your hair. I guess I just realized after driving Thomas to the airport this morning that we haven't seen the rest of you in a while. How's everything going with you all?"

"Oh, fine," said Mary Ann, with just a hint of sarcasm.

Rich looked at her a bit suspiciously. "That's okay, hun. I'm here and I'll listen any time you need to talk."

Mary Ann knew instantly that with children in the room this was not the time to elaborate. "Yep, we're fine," she said again.

They finished their visit a short time later and Karen and Rich headed for the door.

"Thanks for stopping by," Mary Ann said as she held the door for them.

"You all have a great night," Karen told Mary Ann as she walked out.

Rich leaned in to kiss Mary Ann on the cheek, but before he did, he whispered to her, "We're always here if you need to talk."

She hugged him and said, "I know. I love you guys."

That night at bedtime, Mary Ann was tucking Todd into bed.

"Do you want me to read you a story?" she asked him.

"Naw, that's alright."

"Are you sure, Toddy?"

Todd said nothing. He just nodded.

"Alright then. Good night," Mary Ann said and closed the door.

Todd lay in his bed with his arms behind his head, thinking about his grandparents' visit and the stories they each told him about Sparky. With a smile on his face, he closed his eyes and the next thing he knew, he was standing in a field of tall prairie grass. It was a warm, sunny day and he was standing about halfway up a small hill. There were trees off to either side of him, trees behind him but none at the top of the hill. Todd stood still and looked around trying to get his bearings, but this was a place he'd never been before. To get a better view, he began to walk up the hill. Closer to the top, the tall grass suddenly began to move, at first in one line and then it would stop and start again on a different line. And as the movement of the grass got closer, Todd could barely make out the head of a dog. But it didn't seem to be coming towards him. The dog was hopping and peeking over the grass, running a bit and jumping up to get another heading and then, running a little more, he zigged and zagged his way down the hill to where Todd stood. Looking up at him, the dog wagged his tail happily and then sat down next to Todd, with the tip of his tail still wagging. Todd looked at the dog. "Hey there, fella, where did you come from?" But the dog just looked at Todd, tilting his head, and began to pant a little.

Todd crouched down and put the back of his hand out toward the dog's nose. The dog sniffed his hand and gave it two big licks, then stood up and started bounding through the grass again toward the hilltop. When he was about twenty yards away, he stopped and turned back toward Todd, sat down and looked straight at him, then barked calmly and deliberately.

"Woof."

"What is it, boy?"

The dog looked up at the top of the hill, then back to Todd and barked again. "Woof."

"Do you want me to follow you?" Todd asked.

The dog headed up the hill again, only a few yards, before he stopped and looked back at Todd, who was following close behind. The mild breeze brought smells of wild flowers and clover and parted Todd's hair as he jogged up the hill behind his new friend.

When the dog reached the top, he sat down and waited for Todd to catch up. When he did, Todd took a long look around while the dog stayed seated silently at his side. Looking down the other side of the hill, Todd noticed a barbed-wire fence running alongside a gravel road. Across the gravel road was a house and a cabin separated by a large gap where another cabin was under construction. It was this construction site that caught his eye, partly because the framed walls, which were light and looked new, stood out against the dark green leaves of the large oak trees behind it. And partly because it was the only sign of life, as far as Todd could see from the hilltop perch.

Beyond the cabin was a lake and an island, or a point of land. Todd couldn't tell exactly what it was. The gentle breeze now brought with it the smell of fresh cut lumber and the sounds of hammering and an intermittent power saw. Todd could see a man and a boy moving back and forth around the work site. He could also hear some voices fade in and out. As Todd watched the workers, the dog gnawed playfully on a stick he had found, and he stayed right at Todd's feet.

Todd moved down the hill closer to the construction site with the dog following cheerfully, still carrying the stick and wagging his tail. Just when Todd could hear those voices again, they'd stop. As he got closer, Todd clearly heard a voice say, "Okay. What are we gonna need next?"

"Uh, the square, the level, and some 16-penny nails. And a hammer," a boy's voice responded.

"There ya go," said the man who Todd could see now. "You're getting it—alright!" he said to the boy. "Now, let's put that last section up and then we'll have some lunch."

Todd watched intently as the boy hurried to gather the tools and get into position to help the man secure into place a framed section of the wall. When that was done, the young boy ran across the floor, jumped over a sawhorse with an access ramp on it and through a portion of uncompleted exterior wall and into an old pickup, where he retrieved a large cooler, which he brought back to the work floor along with the tools. The man, who Todd assumed was the boy's father, watched this entire athletic performance and just stood with his hands on his hips while shaking his head. Todd was just close enough to make out that the father was smiling wide. Then, he watched as the two sat side by side on a pile of neatly sorted lumber and admired their project so far. Each of them had a sandwich in one hand and a can of pop in the other. They toasted to a job well done by clinking the cans together.

Todd wanted to get closer and maybe even say hello to these two carpenters. But, as he began to move forward, he ran right into the dog and nearly fell over him. Todd caught himself and stood up. He looked down at the dog, who was just sitting and looking up at him with his head cocked to one side. Todd knelt down to pet this shiny black dog. They stared at each other for a long time before Todd looked up to get another view of the workers, but they had disappeared—along with the lumber. Suddenly back in his own bedroom and holding his stuffed bear Benjamin, the next thing Todd heard was the sound of his mother's voice telling him to get ready for school. It was the start of a new day.

*******

When Thomas was on business trips, he'd call home almost every evening and speak to Mary Ann and the children in turn. This time, however, he was particularly interested in talking to Michael.

"So, I understand your teacher is having some issues with you at school," Thomas said in a stern voice. "Do you want to tell me anything about that, Michael?"

"No," he said quietly.

"Not getting homework in on time, smarting off to other boys during class, fighting, being a real tough guy," Thomas remarked. "Is that true?"

"Well, the teacher said it, so it must be true, right?" Michael said in a disrespectful tone.

"I'm asking you, Michael. What's going on?" his father asked, very concerned.

"Those guys are jerks, okay? I was just standing up for myself, alright? That's what I'm supposed to do, isn't it?"

"Yes, in some situations," Thomas agreed. "If someone hits you, for example, or hurts your brother or sister... do you understand?"

"Sure," said Michael curtly. These one-word answers were very irritating to Thomas, and Michael knew it.

"Look!" Michael said, "Those guys had it coming, and I don't understand why you can't just believe me and trust me on this."

"We'll talk about this some more when I get home. But right now, I need you to understand something else," Thomas said. "Your mom needs some help around there, and she can't do everything herself. I expect you to help her," he said angrily and continued barking orders. "The garbage needs to go out. Help with the laundry. Clean your room. And keep that family room and kitchen cleaned up. Do you understand me? You're part of this family, and I expect you to help out and do your share."

"Sure... just like you always do," Michael said in a tone he had never before taken with his father. Then, he handed the phone to Mary Ann and walked off without saying another word.

"Michael. MICHAEL!" Thomas shouted into the phone.

"He's gone, Thomas," Mary Ann said.

"WHAT is wrong with him? Did you hear how he talked to me?"

"Don't worry, I'll talk to him," she said.

"Oh, I'LL talk to him... I'LL TALK TO HIM BY HAND!"

"Just relax," Mary Ann said.

"What do you mean, relax?"

But before Thomas could say another word, Mary Ann said, "He's not entirely wrong, you know."

"WHAT?" Thomas shouted. "I work my butt off out here so that we can have a nice house, and the kids can have the things they want, and we can get ahead of the game for once. And—"

Mary Ann interrupted him. "I understand what you're saying, Thomas, but what *they* see is YOU not here!"

"Hey... I've got some plans and goals for this family, and I'm not just gonna QUIT because things get a little hard once in a while! I just need a little more time!"

"I know, Thomas. Just a little more time and we'll be ahead of the game.

I've been hearing it for 10 years."

"Huh?" Thomas said in surprise. "What do you mean by that?"

"I mean that it doesn't seem to matter what's going on here. It's always just a little more time, or you just gotta get ahead of the game, or there's nothing wrong with hard work. Well, you've just about worked your way right out of this family, Thomas!"

"Okay, okay, I can tell you're upset. We'll talk about it some more when I get home."

"Yes, by all means. When you get home," Mary Ann said coldly.

"I'm sorry you're upset, but I promise you, we'll talk soon."

After an awkward pause, Thomas asked to speak with Jenny.

"Uh... she's not here," Mary Ann said. "She's at the mall with Megan. I'm not sure what she's got going on these days. She's all in a state about what you *do* and *don't do* in the eighth grade. Honestly, Thomas, these girls have all their own little rules about what's *in* and what's *out* and who's *in* and who's *out*. I just can't keep up with it all! She treats me like I'm an idiot!"

"Okay, okay... now... YOU relax," Thomas said. "We'll talk more when I get home," he said in his most reassuring voice. "How about Toddy, is he around?"

"Yes, he's right here," she said and handed Todd the phone.

"Hi, Dad," he said tentatively after hearing half of the heated conversation on his side of the phone.

"Hi, buddy. How are you?"

"Good. Guess what?" Todd said excitedly.

"What?"

"I had a dream last night... a dream with a dog, and he was really friendly, and we ran up this hill, and we watched these guys building a house or something by a lake. It was pretty cool!"

"Oh, that's great, pal. How's school going?"

"Good. I got to sit by Taylor today."

"That's nice, Toddy. Is he good in school?"

"Yeah, he's smart. And the kid at the building was smart, too. He knew all about tools and stuff, and he was a really good runner, too."

"I'm sorry, Toddy. What kid?"

"The kid in my dream. It was just him and this older guy, and they were building a little house or something."

"Ah, I see. Well, I'll have to hear all about it when I get home, okay?"

"Uh, yep, okay."

"Okay, now let me talk to your mother again."

Todd handed the phone to his mother.

"Did you hear that?" Thomas asked Mary Ann.

"Yes," she said through a smile. "I guess those Sparky stories are starting to get to him."

"I guess so," Thomas said smiling. "Okay. Well, that's it for now. I miss you guys. I'll be home Friday night, late," he said.

"Okay, I'll see you then," said Mary Ann. She hung up the phone with a sigh and headed up the stairs.

Thomas sat on the end of his hotel room bed and thought about his family. He had never felt so far away from home. *Why can't they see how important my work is?* he thought. *I'm really onto something here. This one deal—once I make this presentation—could be worth many millions of dollars to the company and ensure my family is well provided for in the years to come.*

Working in the natural gas industry for the last several years, Thomas had recently been focusing on a system that would electronically monitor data from any of his company's customers anywhere in the world. His company, Trans Flow, calibrated large, natural gas flow meters. Since so many of these meters were in such remote locations and technicians to repair these meters were very rare, it took too much time and cost too much money to send someone to each location every time some small problem occurred. And yet, this was how it was being done all over the world. Thomas, however, had figured out a way to monitor these systems without being there. It could be done remotely with computers and satellites. This service would be very valuable to Trans Flow's customers and, therefore, very valuable to Trans Flow. His presentation would explain how Trans Flow could provide a modem to its customers for a small fee, and the customers would agree to pay a monthly fee to have their system monitored—24/7. The company would know immediately what and where the problem was, and many times the technicians could fix it remotely as well. The best part about it was that Thomas' customers had been asking if something like this could be done. And now he had a solution. He was confident that when he presented his idea, it would be received as a great money saver. Also, with his list of nearly 80 customers who had already expressed an interest in buying this type of service, it would be a brilliant solution to solve their problems.

As he sat and thought some more about the whole situation at home, Thomas thought about his family and what Mary Ann had said. He thought about his work and what it was that made him try so hard for each new goal. He remembered the words of his dad, who always said, "A man's gotta take care of his family!"

*What do they want me to do? Quit?* Thomas thought. That very word, quit, was the most disgusting, vomit-inducing word he could ever think of. That was Thomas. He was not afraid of work and was willing to do what it took to provide for his family.

*I am not a quitter,* he thought, then let out a deep sigh and stretched out on the bed in his hotel room with his feet dangling off the end. His father's parting words from the airport came flooding back to him.

*How will you know when you're successful?*

*Are you passionate about your work?*

—

He thought about that second part for a moment. His conclusion was yes. Thomas did enjoy his job, but as he thought about the specifics of it, he realized something he had never considered before. It wasn't actually the job he liked but the solving of interesting problems that he enjoyed.

*Well... that was an interesting epiphany,* he thought. *After all, there are interesting problems everywhere.* The fact was, Thomas had an interesting problem of his own right now. And, as he saw it, the problem entailed several questions that needed to be answered now. *How could I stay at home, or at least in the same town, and still make enough money to support my family?* he pondered. *Could I do something for my current company that would allow this to happen? How could I be a part of this new idea that I've worked on so hard for the last year at Trans Flow?*

Thomas made his decision right then and there. He would tackle the problem the same way he would if it was assigned to him at work. He'd write a list of goals and expectations. He would take notes over the next few weeks as to which questions and ideas he should consider. He would research these questions on fact-finding trips and on the Internet and possibly interview others doing the same thing. *Yeah! I'll do a presentation for myself!*

*******

Todd was in his room getting ready for bed when he heard his mom in the hallway. He saw her in the doorway.

"Hey, Toddy, are you ready for bed?"

"Yeah."

"Did you brush your teeth?"

"I mean, no. I just have to brush my teeth."

"Okay," Mary Ann said smiling. "Todd, are you alright?"

"Yeah, I guess so," he said through a mouth full of toothpaste. "Why?"

"Well, I know you heard some of the arguing on the phone tonight and I wondered how you felt about it."

Todd opened his mouth and dropped a big dollop of foamy toothpaste into the sink with a plop, then looked at her for a moment and said, "I don't like it that Dad's gone all the time. And I know that Michael and Jenny don't like it either. It's always been like that as long as I can remember. But it's different now and I don't know why."

*What an astute observation,* she thought. "Yes, I think it's different now, too. I guess we'll have to think about this some more, you and I, won't we?"

Mary Ann collected her thoughts and asked Todd if he'd like a story.

"Do you know any Sparky stories?" Todd asked.

"You sure like your father's Sparky stories, don't you?" May Ann commented.

"Yeah, but they aren't just stories," Todd said. "They're memories. Sometimes when Dad tells them to me, I can see his eyes get all watery, and sometimes his voice even changes a little, like he can't finish what he wants to say. Do you know what I mean?"

"Yes, I do," Mary Ann replied. "It means your dad is an old softy, and something he's remembering is bringing back old feelings that he had about his dog. I kinda like that about your dad."

"Yeah... me, too," Todd said.

"Now, what should we read?" Mary Ann asked.

"It's okay, Mom. I'm pretty tired."

"Alright, suit yourself. Do you want the door open or closed?"

"Open, a little bit," he said.

"Okay, good night, Toddy," she said as she turned out the light.

"Good night, Mom."

Todd drifted off to sleep quickly that night and was immediately greeted by a small black dog with four white paws and a white tip on the end of his tail. It was the same dog that had led him up the hill and down to watch the carpenters on a summer's day by the lake.

"Sparky? Is that you?" he asked excitedly.

This time the dog came right to him and sat down at Todd's feet. The dog looked up at him with just the end of his tail wagging briskly. He raised his right front paw to shake hands. Todd looked down at the dog but didn't move to shake hands. Then the dog moved his right paw forward and touched Todd's knee.

"Sparky?" Todd said again.

This time, the dog stood up on his hind legs and put his front paws on Todd's thighs and tried to lick him in the face Todd leaned over and held both sides of the dog's face in his hands and knew this was Sparky.

"Sparky!" Todd exclaimed.

This time, the dog got down real low on his front paws with his tail and butt up in the air, wagging and wiggling happily. Then, he bounced from side to side on his front paws and turned circles in front of Todd. He stopped for just a moment—and started all over again. Sparky stood up on his hind legs while Todd held his face. Sparky tried to lick Todd's face again, as though he was a best friend who had been gone for a long time. As the two of them slowly calmed down, Todd pet Sparky in long, firm strokes and thought he was the most well-trained dog he'd ever seen.

"Whatcha doin here, Sparky?" Todd asked again.

Sparky ran several yards away then stopped, looked at Todd, and then looked back in the direction he had been running, then back at Todd once more.

"Okay," Todd said. "Let's go!"

They had been standing on what looked like a gravel road, or a long driveway. As Sparky ran, there was a big brick house to the right that sat in the center of a fenced-in yard and a small field that funneled into the woods on the left. The two ran along a path on the outside of the fenced-in yard toward a river that was just coming into view in front of them. The little dog slowed down when they came to a river and the corner of the fence. Sparky turned right at the end of the fence, walked along the top of the riverbank for a few yards, then stopped and sat down. He looked up at Todd, then to the shoreline of the river. There they saw four boys and a rope swing. They were having a fine time, taking turns jumping off of the swing and swimming in the river.

Todd watched as one boy after the next brought the swing up onto the riverbank and climbed the worn, wooden stepladder tied to the back of the old elm tree. They swung out over the river and, letting go, did their best tricks into the cool water. Todd thought it looked like great fun and started to move towards the boys. Sparky growled slightly and bit at Todd's pant leg, trying to hold him back.

"What's wrong, boy? Don't you want me to go?"

Sparky looked at Todd, happily wagging his tail. So, Todd made another move in the direction of the boys and, again, Sparky growled and snapped at the cuff of his pants.

"Okay, okay, I get it. I'll stay here," Todd said.

The two sat quietly on the riverbank and watched the boys play. Todd couldn't help noticing a few things. First, even though he and Sparky were pretty close to these boys who were swimming, none of them even noticed Todd or Sparky. Second, there was another dog playing with the boys that looked exactly like Sparky. And last, in the area where the boys were swimming, Todd thought there must have been a pretty big hole because they would swing out, do a flip or some other trick and then swim just a few yards and stand right up in the river where the water was only up to their waists. He thought that it was very unusual for someone to jump from a rope swing and land into a spot deep enough, but then be able to stand up in shallow water so quickly.

Sparky barked a quiet little "woof" and looked past the fence towards the woods where he walked down the narrow path, stopping only for a moment to make sure Todd was following. As Todd trotted down the path to catch up to Sparky, he brushed away the branches that fell across the path in front of him. He closed his eyes as more and more branches crossed the path in front of his face and lost sight of Sparky.

The next thing he knew, he was in his bed under the covers, brushing the blankets from one side to the other. When he realized where he was, he reached up and put both arms over his head, flopping the covers down to his waist with one big "Humff!"

Todd lay there for a while, remembering everything he had seen in the most vivid dream he'd ever had. He thought about it for some time, then smiled and knew he would remember it always.

## 6

The next morning, Todd sat down to eat his breakfast with the normal taunts from Michael. This time, though, it didn't even faze him. He simply smiled at his brother and said, "If you say so, Mike."

Todd was still thinking about his evening with Sparky when Jenny came down to breakfast. He thought she smelled like oranges. Clearly some new *in* cologne or body wash, he figured. He also thought she was acting suspiciously. Todd didn't miss much, and most of the time he couldn't care less about what his sister did or didn't do, but this interested him. He noticed that she was completely ready for school, and her book bag was right next to her chair, looking heavier than normal. Usually, it would be left by the front door. She also kept looking at the clock. This wasn't so unusual, but she was already a full 15 minutes early—and that just never happens!

After Jenny wolfed down a slice of peanut butter toast and a glass of juice, she ran out the side door.

*Hmmm,* Todd thought. *I'll have to keep my eye on this one.*

Todd left for school without mentioning anything about his dream. When he returned home, his sister was right behind him, dressed differently than when she left for school that morning. She was now wearing makeup and a totally new outfit. She quickly ran upstairs and came down wearing her regular clothes again. The makeup had disappeared.

"So, what's with the makeup?" Todd asked. "Aren't you beautiful enough already?" he said mockingly.

Jenny shot him a look of disdain. "That's none of your concern, you little mutant!"

Todd stared back at her with a smirk on his face. Then, the front door flew open and immediately slammed shut. It was Michael. And he was obviously upset. His jacket was torn and dirty. He had a scrape on his left cheek and a scrape on his right knee. His jeans were ripped and he was bleeding slightly.

"Don't say anything about this to Mom!" he said, pointing a finger at his siblings. The look was unmistakable. This was serious and he meant it.

As soon as they heard the garage door begin to open, Michael bolted up the stairs. Mary Ann and Reggie came into the kitchen from the garage. They were laughing and talking about some upcoming event at the museum. Todd hadn't heard his mother's laugh in a while, but for some reason he wasn't sure he liked it.

Reggie set down a large box of books on the counter. He turned and saw Todd in the doorway and said, "Hey… how's my favorite art connoisseur?"

"Fine," Todd said coldly and left the kitchen.

Reggie's eyebrows knitted together, wondering what that look was for. In the other room, Todd overheard his mother asking Reggie to stay for supper. He held his breath, waiting for Reggie's answer.

"I'd love to," Reggie replied.

"Great," said Mary Ann.

"Anything I can do to help?" Reggie asked as she got out a large pot for the spaghetti.

"Yes. You can open that nice bottle of Chardonnay in the fridge, and what do you know about garlic bread?"

Reggie smiled and said, "I know I don't like it too crispy."

"Neither do I. So, I'll put you in charge of making the bread," Mary Ann said.

"You shan't be disappointed, m'lady," Reggie said in his best British accent.

Mary Ann giggled. "Oh sir, you're so gallant," she replied in her best British accent as they both laughed again.

Todd and Jenny had heard everything from the family room. He looked at his sister and rolled his eyes. She turned up a sneer on one side of her face and nodded in silent agreement.

Soon the smell of garlic bread filled the main floor, and even though Todd wasn't Reggie's biggest fan, he couldn't wait to taste the spaghetti, tossed salad, garlic bread, and wine—for the adults.

"More wine?" Mary Ann asked Reggie.

"Well, maybe just one more glass," he said as he held out his glass for Mary Ann to fill. "Wonderful dinner, Mary Ann. Just excellent!" complimented Reggie.

Jenny shot Todd an eye-rolling look and Todd confirmed her displeasure with a slight incline of his head. Michael, who had cleaned himself up pretty well, had been very quiet all throughout dinner. He had covered the mark on his cheek with some make-up, doing a fair job of it, too. He sat in a chair next to his mom in such a way that she could only see the right side of his face. Even Jenny was impressed, which was hard to do. She kept craning her neck at the table to try and get a better look at Michael's cheek.

Mary Ann was so busy laughing and talking with Reggie that she didn't notice either Jenny or Michael and his bruise. When the adults finished their meal, Reggie offered to help clear the table while giving Mary Ann more compliments about how good everything was, which kept the eye rolling between Jenny and Todd at an all-time high.

Reggie said good night and kissed Mary Ann on both cheeks, like in the movies, and she gave him a playful swat on the shoulder and told him not to be so dramatic. "We're not in Europe, you know," Mary Ann said.

"Oh, I forgot. It must be the ambiance," Reggie said with a grin.

"What is he, French now?" Jenny leaned over and whispered to Todd.

Todd didn't know exactly what she meant, but he nodded in agreement with a disapproving look on his face, just the same.

After Reggie left, Mary Ann continued cleaning up the kitchen, humming as she worked. It seemed as if everyone had gone to neutral corners. Michael was upstairs in his room, Jenny was on the computer, and Todd was at the dining room table doing his homework.

When the phone rang, Mary Ann jumped a little. She answered it with a shake of her head. *How silly*, she thought. *It's just the phone.* "Hello?"

"Hey, it's me," Thomas said. "How's it going at home?"

"Oh, good. We just finished supper."

"Oh, yeah? What'd you have?"

"Spaghetti. Reggie stopped by and ate with us. You remember Reggie, right?"

"Ah... yeah, your art friend from the museum, right?"

"Yep, that's the one. Do you want to talk to Todd? He's right here."

"Ah, sure, put him on."

"Toddy. Here. Your dad's on the phone."

Thomas thought... *well, yeah, I want to talk to Todd, but I'd like to talk to my wife first.*

"Hi, Dad," Todd said. "How are you?"

"I'm good, Toddy. Are you taking care of your mom while I'm gone?"

"Ye-ah," Todd said through a big smile. It made him feel good and kind of important, even though he knew his dad was mostly kidding.

"So, Todd, did anything good happen to you today?"

"No, just school. But guess what, Dad?"

"What?"

"I had a dream last night about Sparky!"

"You did? How did you know it was Sparky?"

"He was all shiny black and had four white paws and a white nose—I mean muzzle—and he had a white tip on the end of his tail."

"Yep," Thomas said. "That sounds like Sparky."

This gave Thomas a wonderful feeling. He was sure that his son was having nice dreams because of the stories he had told him.

"I saw four boys swimming in a river and jumping from a rope swing," Todd told Thomas.

"Yeah, we used to do that all the time in the summer," Thomas said. "There was a great spot over the Sauk River behind Mike Tise's house."

Todd then told his dad about the boys doing flips and tricks and teasing each other as they went off the swing. He told him how one Sparky had led him to the swimming spot and stayed with him, and how another Sparky played with the boys, swimming and barking at them and trying to catch them by their old tennis shoes before they could swing into the water. Todd also told him about running down the path after Sparky and brushing branches out of the way until they turned into his bed covers.

"Oh... that sounds like a really good dream, buddy. Did you like it?"

"Yeah, it was great!"

"Well... I'll tell you what, Toddy. We'll talk some more about this when I get home on Friday, okay?"

"Okay." And with that, Todd hung up the phone.

*Augh! I sort of wanted to talk to the rest of my family, too,* thought

Thomas, but it was okay because he still had a great feeling from talking to Todd. Shaking his head, he thought to himself, *Two Sparky's, what an imagination... Hmm... I don't remember telling Todd about the rope swing.*

"Todd," Mary Ann said. "Did you have a nice talk with your father?"

"Yah."

"Didn't he want to talk to me?" she asked, wondering why Thomas was being such a jerk.

"Nope," he replied, then headed upstairs.

Todd decided to go to bed early that night. He could hear the smile in his father's voice when they talked about his dream on the phone and thought it would be a good idea to try to find Sparky one more time. So, he climbed into bed and scooted down under the blankets much lower than normal, and tried to position himself precisely where he had been the last time he dreamed about Sparky. As he lay awake, he thought about his family. He wondered what actually happened to Michael. He thought about Jenny and why she was being so sneaky. He wondered about his father. He wondered why he couldn't find a way to spend more time at home. He also wondered what would happen when his father returned from his business trip. There had been lots of cross words exchanged during his last call home, and Todd was concerned that things were getting worse for his family. *Dad is gone all the time, Michael is fighting, Jenny is doing something she knows is wrong, and Mom seemed happiest when she is with Reggie.*

# 7

Mary Ann worried that Todd may be ill since he had gone to bed earlier than usual. "Toddy, are you okay?" she asked as she entered his room and sat beside him on his bed.

"Yeah, I'm okay, Mom," he replied as he resurfaced from under the covers.

Mary Ann brushed his hair back on his forehead and caressed his face. "Did something happen at school today?" she asked. "Anything you want to talk about?" She brushed her hand across his forehead again and kissed him there to make sure he didn't have a fever.

Todd smiled and gave her the look that he'd seen his father use many times… the one where he tipped his head down and then looked up at her from above his reading glasses. It was a look that meant *I'm fine. I'm sure I'm fine. And thank you for your concern, but I'm fine.*

"Okay, I'll leave you to your dreams," Mary Ann said to Todd, who was hoping she'd leave so he could get on with his plan to meet Sparky.

Todd dozed off, but this time he could not figure out where sleep came in and Sparky appeared. He was just suddenly there! On his bedroom floor, calmly wagging his tail. "Hey boy, how ya doing?" Todd exclaimed. Sparky jumped up onto the bed and licked Todd's face. "Where should we go tonight, boy?" he asked Sparky while briskly petting him on both sides of his neck and face.

With a tug on the bed covers, Sparky looked up and the whole bed turned 180 degrees. When it stopped, they were at the high school looking at Michael, who was sitting on the floor alone at the end of a dark hallway, leaning against the lockers and staring blankly.

"Hey, Mike! What are you doing?" Todd said. Michael didn't move. "Oh yeah. This is a dream, right Sparky?" Todd said out loud.

They looked at each other for just a moment and then back at Michael. He sat there, with no homework, no journal, no humming a tune. And Michael, who loved music, was always humming or whistling some part of a song he was working on.

A couple of girls came around the corner and almost tripped on Michael's legs. "Excuse me," said one of the girls, but Michael barely looked up.

Todd and Sparky were still on the bed as it took them on a magic carpet ride following the girls down the hallway. Though Todd knew he was only a passenger on this ride, with no control of where it would go or how fast or how he could stop it, he wasn't scared with Sparky by his side.

They followed the girls a bit more. "Do you believe that?" the girl said to her friend. "I said, 'excuse me,' and he didn't even say a word."

"Yeah, what a jerk," the other girl said. "I used to think he was cool."

"I know, but now he just sits and stares and doesn't talk to anyone anymore."

"Yeah, it's like he's on drugs or someone died or something."

"Well, whatever... he doesn't care about anything, so why should we care about him, or what he thinks?"

The girls shook their heads in agreement.

Todd was shocked. He always thought his brother was a jerk only to him but not to cute girls at school, and not on purpose. In fact, Todd had noticed how easy it seemed for Michael to talk to girls and how he had friends from many different school groups: jocks, theater kids, math kids, art kids and music groups. Everyone got along with Michael. Yet Todd, too, had noticed Michael's sullen behavior and was a little afraid for his brother. *Could he really be in that kind of trouble?* he thought.

As the girls headed into their classroom, the bed glided toward the main entrance of the school, where it pressed through the double doors and into White Birch Mall. Jenny had been there with her friends the day before. Floating past the brightly lit stores and colorful signs, Todd and Sparky enjoyed the smells of popcorn and pretzels in the air.

When the magic carpet-like bed came to a stop, they were behind Jenny and her three friends. Todd knew Jenny and Megan but didn't recognize the other friends. Their names were Amber and Sarah. Amber was clearly the boss of this operation. They were all talking at the same time and Todd couldn't make sense of anything they were saying. Then, right in front of Grunwald & Kiger Fine Jewelers, the bed came to an abrupt stop. Even though they hadn't been going very fast, Todd lurched forward from his seated position and landed flat on his face with his chin just over the foot of the bed. He was nose to butt with Amber Jackson. Todd quickly scrambled backward, like a crab, to the center of the bed and looked around red-faced to see if anyone had noticed. *Of course, they hadn't. No one can see us or hear us at all,* he laughed to himself.

Todd could see that Jenny and Megan were heading into Carlson's Shoes when Amber stopped them, hands on her hips.

"You two go ahead and look at shoes a little while," Amber ordered. "But don't forget to meet us in the food court with the makeup and stuff that you're going to steal for us. If you want to hang with us, then that's your initiation."

Megan gave Jenny a quick and unmistakable disapproving look before turning to Amber and nodding obediently.

"Yeah, just the stuff on the list," Sarah added. That's my favorite."

Amber and Sarah smiled deviously at each other. "We're going to look at some earrings. We'll meet you at the food court at 4:30."

Todd was stunned. His eyes where as big as goose eggs, and he hung his mouth wide open in disbelief. When the girls parted ways, he assumed that he and Sparky would follow his sister, but the bed jumped to the right to follow Amber and Sarah straight into Grunwald & Kiger. Now he could clearly hear the conversation, and he didn't like what he heard.

"Why do we have to be here with those two again?" Sarah asked Amber.

"I told you. I just want to get close enough to Jenny, long enough for me to get her brother Mike to notice me. And in the meantime, we get free stuff!"

"But I don't like being seen with those two. They're so... un-cool, you know?"

"Yeah, I know. But they have been getting better since they've been hanging out with us," Amber said with a smirk.

"Well... how could they not?" Sarah agreed.

Todd was furious! These girls weren't Jenny's friends! All that stuff he had noticed about Jenny... the makeup, the orange-scented body wash, the kind of clothes she wore now... that was all Amber Jackson's doing. And now she was having Jenny steal for her!

Todd was livid with them, but he was angry with Jenny, too. He wasn't going to let her off the hook just because she was pressured into it. Todd had never experienced a feeling like this before. He wanted revenge on someone who had wronged his sister, and he wasn't sure what to make of it. He had never even dreamed of hitting a girl before but felt Amber had it coming. He wanted to stomp right over there and tell that witch to stay away from his sister, or else.

Before he could make a move, though, the bed took off again, and Todd grabbed the blankets with both hands. They were heading straight towards the down escalator and over the edge. His eyes grew wider and wider until the foot of the bed was hanging right over the escalator steps. He held on tight and shut his eyes.

The bed stopped moving and Todd opened his eyes to find himself back in his room alone on his bed. Everything was back to normal, except for that awful witch, Amber. Todd knew that Sparky had shown him a real event even though he couldn't prove it.

*******

72

The next morning Todd bounded into the kitchen, where Michael and Jenny were already having breakfast. The smell of toast and Mary Ann's coffee filled the air. "Guess what?" Todd said excitedly.

Michael and Jenny looked at him for a moment in silence. "WHAT?" they finally said in unison and with fake enthusiasm.

"I met Dad's dog last night, and it wasn't the first time either." Todd said this with a huge smile on his face.

Michael and Jenny looked at each other without saying a word. Then they both looked at Todd and burst out laughing.

"Whatever, dude," said Michael, who went back to eating his cereal.

"Seriously?" Jenny said, shaking her head.

Michael and Jenny listened as Todd spoke, but only because they hadn't finished their breakfast yet. Undaunted, Todd began to recount his first meetings with Sparky, detailing much of what he had seen. He left out the events with Amber Jackson and Jenny's makeup heist and the two girls who were talking about Michael. Todd thought he should keep that to himself for a while. He wasn't sure if he would use the information to bolster his story about Sparky, or if he may need it as ammunition against Michael and Jenny in some future encounter.

As Todd waited for the school bus that morning, he continued to smile as he thought about the little black dog. He decided not to mention it for a while, especially since his brother and sister didn't believe any of it anyway. Todd just sat and listened to Jenny, who was talking to one of her new friends about who liked whom, and who was hot, and so on. Michael was scribbling in a notebook, perhaps some words to a song he had been thinking about. Michael had kept a notebook for a couple of years now, with song ideas, lyrics and poems, or maybe just a phrase he liked that would turn into something later.

Todd watched his brother write, and even though he didn't know what he wrote, Todd knew it made his brother happy. It was important to him. Todd was happy seeing his brother like this, but he wasn't sure why. Michael had been a total jerk to him for a long time, teasing him relentlessly, but this still made him smile. He was also happy because today was Thursday, and that meant only one more day until his father came home. In Todd's mind, everything would be better when his father got home.

Todd thought hard, wishing there was a way to make Michael believe that Sparky was real, or at least more than a dream. Still waiting for the bus, Todd decided it was now or never. He began, very calmly and quietly, telling Michael everything he had seen in the dream the night before and everything the girls had said about Michael. When he had finished, Michael was staring at Todd with his mouth open in disbelief.

"WHAT?" Michael gasped. "How do you know all that? Do you have some kind of spy deal worked out with one of your little buddy's brothers or sisters?"

"Nope, but that's a pretty good idea," Todd said with a quizzical look.

"THEN HOW?" Michael barked.

"Sparky," Todd replied. "He's here for a reason. I'm just not sure what it is yet, but I just know he's trying to tell me something."

"That's just crazy. It's not possible," Michael said.

"Michael?" Todd said.

"What?"

"Those girls, they... they said you were so different, you might be on drugs or something. Is that true?"

"WHAT? No!"

"But you are different... you're so quiet. You were rude to those girls. That's just not you... just tell me what's happened."

Michael looked at Todd for a long moment, deciding what he would say. Then, with a big sigh he said, "Okay... remember the other night when I came home with my jeans ripped, with that bruise on my cheek?"

"Yeah, what happened?"

"I got in a fight with someone who was supposed to be my friend," Michael said. "Not only that, but he's the captain of my swim team—Dale Brody. He's supposed to set an example for everyone on the team, but he's a total jerk."

"What did he do?" Todd asked.

"He tried to get me to smoke pot, Toddy. And when I told him no, he said that just wasn't going to work for him. We were in the back of the swim team bus, and he and a couple of his buddies got around me and pinned me in one of the back seats against the window. He was behind me, and he leaned over the seat putting his elbow on my left shoulder and against my neck. Then, he leaned down hard on it and told me that I was going to smoke pot so that he and his pals could be sure I wouldn't tell on them. I told him that I was going to tell on them right that minute if he didn't back off and leave me alone. Then, he slammed my head into the window with his elbow."

"What did your coach do?" Todd asked.

"Well, Coach Vance was just getting on the bus, so we couldn't really do anything else about it at that point. And when we got off the bus, that's when he told me if I didn't smoke with them he and his two sidekicks were going to give me a beating once a week until I did. Then, he punched me in the stomach and knocked me down. That's when the other two joined in, and each of them took turns kicking me a few times before they left, laughing the whole way. So, the only time I could stand up for myself was in class, when there was a teacher around. That's why I was acting up in class. I wasn't going to let them humiliate me in front of the other kids, too. That's why I was so mad at Dad. He just totally assumed that I had done something wrong!"

"Wow, Michael, what are you going to do?" Todd asked.

Michael smiled and said, "It's already done. I wrote three anonymous letters. One to Coach Vance, one to the principal, and one to Brody's parents. The letters stated that I was a concerned parent whose child was smoking marijuana that he had gotten from Dale. And guess what? Two days later, Coach Vance called a special swim practice. Everyone had to be there. So, I get there, and guess who's there?"

"Who?"

"The principal, Coach Vance, Brody's parents, a couple of other parents, and a policeman with a German Shepard on a leash. They all wanted to know who had been smoking marijuana with Dale. Of course, one of his buddies caved right away and started saying how Dale MADE him do it. Then, two other guys chimed right in and were also pointing the finger straight at Dale. So, he's suspended from school, and it looks like his folks are going to put him somewhere else in a different school."

"Wow, Michael, I'm glad he's gone!" Todd said. "How did you know what to do? How did you get the idea about the letters?"

"You know how Dad is always saying we should just think it through, plan our next move and think again?"

"Yeah," Todd replied.

"Well, that's what I did. I didn't want to ask him about it so I just thought about it instead and made a plan."

Then Michael smiled and said, "Toddy?" And Michael never called Todd *Toddy*.

Todd looked suspiciously at Michael for a moment and said, "Yeah?"

"I don't know if you've noticed this or not, but I haven't picked on you or teased you one time since the day I came home with my cheek bruised and my jeans ripped. So, I guess you can thank Dale for that. I wanted to say that I didn't like being bullied when it happened to me, so... I just wanted to tell you I'm sorry, okay?"

"Ah... yeah, okay," Todd said with a bewildered look on his face. He didn't quite know what to make of this, but he liked it.

*******

That night, the Preston kids were on their own for supper. Mary Ann had put Michael in charge. Todd wasn't sure if he liked the idea but thought this might be a good chance to see if Michael was sincere about his apology. Mary Ann had made it very clear that she wouldn't be out too late. She and Reggie had to finalize some details over dinner for the museum's art fair, which was coming up in two weeks.

Todd sat quietly at the kitchen table and ate his portion of the frozen pizza his brother and sister had cooked. Jenny made little comments to Michael about Reggie and their last dinner together. "Dinner meetings, huh," Jenny said. "What's up with that?"

Michael just looked at Jenny, raised one eyebrow, then looked at Todd and motioned towards him with his head. Jenny understood. She understood that she wasn't to say any more about Reggie and their mother in front of Todd. But he didn't notice his siblings at all. He was busy thinking about how he would tell his father about Sparky when he returned the following night.

Meanwhile, at the museum, Reggie waited for a delivery man to drop off two orders of Peking Duck, which he knew was Mary Ann's favorite. Reggie took the orders from Minn Choe, his friend from Tommy Chan's House of China, along with two bottles of Lora Donna wine, which Minn had picked up at Reggie's request. Reggie paid the bill and tipped Minn a twenty for his prompt, efficient service. Then, he headed for the break room, where he tucked the food and wine into the mini-fridge and went about setting the table for dinner.

In the museum were many fine displays and works of art from all over America, mainly from the 1880s to present day. There were also entire rooms of historical significance. There was a doctor/dentist office from the early 1900s, a soda fountain from the 1950s, and a completely furnished replica of Martin and Rosemary Danforth's Victorian parlor. Martin Danforth was one of the town's founding fathers. He and his wife were quite the aristocrats in their day. They hosted a great number of visiting dignitaries and politicians and were in with anyone of means in the entire tri-state area in the 1920s.

The room was beautiful, with elaborately carved high-back chairs and camel-back sofas covered in the most luxurious fabrics of the day. Rich leathers, red velvets, blue satins, and silks covered much of the furnishings. Fine patterned rugs from Persia were on the floors and beautiful tapestries on the walls. Oil portraits of the Danforths themselves hung in a place of honor above the great fireplace.

The room also boasted famous paintings by Titian and Caravaggio in ornately carved and gilded frames. A clear statement to any educated soul, that this family, at least in Mr. Danforth's mind, was equal to any in history thus far.

The fireplace was magnificent, though it was no longer functional. However, the oil lamps and candles throughout the room were. It was this room that Reggie chose for the evening's dining experience.

Mary Ann arrived promptly at six. Reggie escorted her to the office where they'd worked and planned many times before. They began by organizing the tasks that needed to be done before the show. Each took turns writing notes and laying out who should do each task and by what time.

"We need to contact radio and newspaper and give the okay to run the announcements," Mary Ann said.

"Who's going to set the layout for the artists' booths at Central Park? And by what time?" Reggie asked. "We also need to call the Police Department and hire one extra officer to patrol during the show."

"Yes, and we'll need to call the City Parks and Recreation Department to set out extra garbage cans," Mary Ann said. "Also, we have to make sure the Porta Potty people have them set into place the night before."

Moving right along with their decision-making, the two were joking and teasing each other the whole time. When they would momentarily disagree, one would say, "Flip a coin," or "I'll rock, paper, scissors you for it." Then, they would decide, laugh and move on.

"Hey! I'm hungry. Weren't you going to buy me dinner?" Mary Ann asked with mock alarm while swatting Reggie on the shoulder.

Reggie smiled. "Uh… sure. Let me see if I can scare up a couple of Cokes and some granola bars."

"Oooh… big spender," replied Mary Ann with a laugh.

"Why don't you just finish up that last bit about the Boy Scouts on the cleanup crew and I'll be right back."

Reggie hurried to the break room where he carefully placed each order of Peking Duck onto two of the Danforth's finest china dinner plates and reheated each of them in the microwave. Then, he uncorked one of the bottles of wine, poured some into two tall glasses of hand-cut crystal stemware and placed them on the small but highly polished walnut table. He lit several of the room's beautiful crystal oil lamps and candles before retrieving the entrées from the break room.

Looking up from her work, Mary Ann frowned slightly, wondering where he had gone. When Reggie came into view, she saw him standing in the arched doorway of the parlor with one arm behind his back, his nose in the air and gesturing with the other hand.

"Dinner is served," he said in his most ostentatious voice.

Mary Ann turned up one side of her mouth. "Whatever," she said as she rolled her eyes and shook her head. "Ummm, something smells good," she added, walking toward the parlor.

Surprised at the sight when she entered the room, she stood with her mouth wide open. "Oh, my gosh! This is awesome!" she said. "This is wonderfully elegant. The only thing missing is a real butler!"

Reggie stood poised to seat her and push in her chair. "Yeah, why not take a little advantage of a place like this when you have a chance?"

Mary Ann had seen this room many times before in the daylight. But at night, with the candles and oil lamps burning, it was simply beautiful. She couldn't stop looking around and noticing every little detail about the room. It was as if she had gone back in time.

"Ooooh, Peking Duck! My favorite! Wow, this is way better than a granola bar! And I'm starving!"

They talked, ate and laughed, and all Mary Ann's worries and troubles magically disappeared. They drank wine and toasted the Danforths and then each other. They pretended they were rich and famous and wondered about the Danforths and their celebrity status. They wondered who the Danforths' friends were and what those conversations must have been like back in their time, and they drank until there was just one more splash of wine in the second bottle.

By now, Reggie and Mary Ann were sitting very close and looking into each other's eyes. Reggie smiled, and Mary Ann smiled back. Then, Reggie kissed her. It was a soft, warm kiss. Mary Ann kissed him back, and in that instant, the clarity of reality hit her like a punch in the stomach. Everything came rushing back. She wasn't a celebrity from the 1920s. She wasn't living in this beautiful home. And she wasn't dining with her husband. She *was*, however, still kissing Reggie.

Mary Ann put both hands on Reggie's shoulders and pushed him away. She held him at arm's length for a few seconds and said out loud, "OH MY GOSH! Reggie! I can't do this! I'm married!"

Reggie was startled, and now his eyes were open—nearly as wide as Mary Ann's. "I... I'm sorry, Mary Ann. I just, uh... I was in the moment and it seemed so natural. I never meant to hurt you... or offend you at all... I'm sorry," Reggie stammered.

Mary Ann looked around the room, as if she suddenly didn't remember where she was. She looked down at her chair and back to the table, then up at Reggie again. She looked for her purse, but it was still in the office.

Then, she looked at Reggie in the chest. She didn't want to look him in the eye. "I have to go! I can't talk about this right now," she said firmly.

Mary Ann started for the office but turned and looked around the room one more time, remembering the fantasy she had just experienced. Her eyebrows knitted together. Now, she did look Reggie in the eye and asked, "Did you plan this Reggie?"

"I—" Reggie began.

But Mary Ann put both hands up, and with palms out, she looked down and to the side.

Reggie stopped instantly, dead in his tracks, with his mouth still open.

"NO! I can't talk about this right now," Mary Ann said. She scurried through the office and snatched her purse off the back of the chair and was gone out the front door.

Reggie plopped down in one of the dining chairs. "Whoa… that wasn't quite the ending I had pictured in my mind," he said.

Mary Ann drove home, overwhelmed with conflicting feelings. She didn't like herself very much right now. She never thought she would ever do anything like this. She liked Reggie very much, just not right now. She wondered if he had planned for that to happen.

*What was he thinking?* she thought.

Mary Ann wasn't very happy with Thomas right now either, come to think of it. If Thomas wasn't always in some other state, she would be having dinner with him. But, she did do something like this, and now she felt terrible about it. She didn't like crying because it made her feel weak, but she was crying. With her eyes blurry, she found it difficult to focus as she drove home. She just wanted to stop and think, but she had already told the kids she'd be home early.

Mary Ann blamed Reggie. *This whole stupid mess is his fault. Maybe it isn't all his fault... I did kiss him, too. No... It was the wine!* she thought, as she made her way towards home on the rain-soaked streets.

The streetlights and neon signs reflected off the wet roads, making it even more difficult to focus. "Darn it, Thomas!" she said out loud. "You're not blameless in this either. You're never home."

Mary Ann tried to think of the last time she and her husband had a nice dinner together when she was jolted by a loud H O N K!! A pickup truck, with its engine revving and horn blaring, flew right in front of her as she absentmindedly coasted through a red light. It missed her car by mere inches, forcefully spraying the windshield with water from the rainy intersection. It sent her car skidding clockwise 180 degrees.

The car slammed into the curb on the right side of the street and was now facing oncoming traffic. Mary Ann's heart was racing and panic set in as she grabbed the gearshift, jamming the car into reverse and hitting the gas. Her wet tires whirred and smoked and pulled her back slowly before catching the curb and jolting her backwards onto the abandoned sidewalk and out of harm's way. The driver of the pickup never stopped. After all, she had been the one who ran the red light.

Now, the line of cars that had been behind her crawled slowly by. As they passed, all the people gawked at her through the dripping wet glass. Mary Ann wondered if they were trying to determine if she was alright, or maybe they just wanted to see the idiot who had run the red light. She was glad for the rain now. It helped hide her tear-soaked face from the onlookers. She felt embarrassed and scared but thankful no one had been hurt.

One by one, a procession of onlookers passed until she had a clear section of road to pull her car off the sidewalk and back onto State Street. She was wide awake now, heart pounding against her ribs and adrenalin surging up her spine. Mary Ann was petrified, mostly at the thought of what might have happened. She found the nearest open parking lot, pulled in and stopped the car. She looked around, and finding herself alone, she began to sob.

Mary Ann cleaned herself up the best she could and continued her drive home. She entered through the garage, like always, and pretended that nothing had happened. She was a bit late but nothing too unusual. She turned off the overhead lights as she came into the family room where the kids were watching TV.

"Time for bed," she announced, making sure the lights were down low in case there were any telltale signs that she'd been crying.

Aside from the usual bedtime groans, nothing seemed out of the ordinary.

# 8

Todd was first up the stairs and into bed, hoping he'd fall asleep quickly. Pulling the covers up and placing them around his chest, he was surprised to see Sparky, plain as day, right on his own bed. It was as though he had just closed his eyes for a second and Sparky was there.

"Hey boy, how ya doing?"

Sparky wagged his tail briskly. As Todd leaned forward to pet the dog, Sparky licked his face enthusiastically. "Where are we going tonight, boy?" Todd asked.

Sparky hopped off the bed and waited for Todd, who sat up and saw Sparky sitting calmly on the floor, pointing with one raised paw at one of the strangest things Todd had ever seen. There in his bedroom, hovering about a foot off the ground, was a wavy window of air.

Todd felt as if he was looking through the hot air of a jet engine at the airport, or looking at someone across a campfire. But the air wasn't moving in any one direction. It was just wavy.

Todd's mouth fell open as he began to examine it. He got up close and pushed it with his hand. It jiggled like a movie screen and felt like a heavy quilt on a clothesline, though he could see straight through it with only minor distortions. He looked at Sparky, who was patiently waiting for Todd to finish his examination. He pushed it again, then looked at his fingers and rubbed them together. They didn't sting or hurt in any way. He sniffed them but they didn't smell any different than they normally did, yet he had no idea what to make of this thing.

Sparky, on the other hand, knew exactly what to do. He barked one mellow "woof," cocked his head and waited for Todd to look at him. When he did, Sparky ran and jumped into the wavy window of air and waited for Todd, who could see him, right there sitting inside this strange wavy thing, wagging his tail. Todd put his hand on it again and gave it a shove. This time, his hand and arm went right through, with a sort of a muffled pop. Todd stood there in disbelief, looking at his hand on the inside of this wavy window, then he smiled because it felt like puffs of air, or feathers on his skin. Sparky barked again and Todd knew it was time to go. He took a deep breath, closed his eyes and pushed his way through. He was amazed when he opened his eyes and Sparky was right there to greet him.

The window opened to a tunnel about twenty yards long. Once inside, the waviness was gone. The watery jelly was replaced with normal air but with definite edges, like a clear plastic tube. Todd discovered he could breathe just fine. In fact, he thought it smelled like his father's cologne. Todd stood for just a moment and looked at his arms. His skin was moving in waves, in the same way it did when he and his friends would put the vacuum on in reverse and blow the hose on their skin.

Sparky waited for Todd to get his bearings, then jumped right out the other side of the tunnel. Todd followed and, again, he felt the little pop as he went through. It was much like the popping of a thick soap bubble, but it was almost as though it came from inside him and not the edge of the window. At first, he saw his sister, who was nicely dressed and sitting in a low-back chair in a beautiful home, with a notebook, a microphone and lots of TV cameras. She was interviewing Oprah Winfrey!

"Cut! Cut!" a producer yelled. "Where did this kid come from? He's in the shot!"

"It's alright, Randy. It's okay, he's my brother."

"Okay, Miss Preston... ahh... take five, everybody," the producer said as crew members from every corner dropped their gear and began walking off to the left.

"Excuse me, Miss Winfrey. I need to talk to my little brother for a minute," Jenny said.

"Sure, Jen," Oprah replied. "Take your time."

"Toddy, what are you doing here? I have an important interview."

Todd smiled and said, "No you don't. But you've got a great dream going on, I see."

"What do you mean, dream?"

Instantly, Jenny looked around and saw she was sitting on the edge of her bed in her flowery flannel pajamas in her very own bedroom.

"What the heck?!" she said.

"I brought someone to meet you," Todd said.

He motioned to Sparky who sat politely at Todd's side and looking attentively at Jenny. He cocked his head and wagged his tail briskly and was very cute.

"Oh my gosh! He's real!" Jenny exclaimed. "He's so cute. Can I pet him?" she asked.

"Sure," Todd said. "He's such a great dog and smart, too. Come on! He wants to show us something."

"I can't believe it!" Jenny said, shaking her head the whole time. "Wait, what do you mean, the dog wants to show us something?"

"His name is Sparky, and I don't know how I know, I just know, okay?" Todd said.

"Ah... I guess... so, what do we do now?" Jenny asked.

"I think we have to get Michael, too. Is that right, Sparky?"

Sparky gave a little downward nod, with a little puff of breath. One couldn't really call it a bark, but the message was clear just the same.

"Okay, boy," Todd said. "Let's go get Michael."

Immediately, Sparky ran out the door and down the hall to Michael's room, with Todd and Jenny following right behind. When they got to his room, the door was shut. Sparky pointed his nose directly at the doorknob. Todd opened the door, and again, there was the hovering wavy window of air that he had experienced earlier.

"AHH!" Jenny moaned in terror as she fell back against the opposite wall of the hallway, cowering on the floor in fear. "Uh, what the heck is THAT?"

Normally, Todd would have teased the pants off her for this, but this time he simply smiled and took her hand and said, "It's okay. Michael is dreaming. And it's a way to jump into his dream with him."

"WHAT! Are you kidding me? How do you know that?" Jenny asked.

Todd replied, "I've been through one before. It's how Sparky and I got into your dream with Oprah, Miss Preston."

"Watch," he said as he stuck his arm right through the wavy window and waved at her from inside it.

Jenny stood in awe with her mouth open and watched in disbelief as Todd swung his arm all around. Wherever he moved it, the hole in the waves would follow and stay tight around his arm. Then he motioned to her to come and she could see the skin on his arm move as it had before. With that, Jenny Preston passed out.

"Oh brother. We don't have time for this," Todd said as he knelt on the floor, pushing her onto her back and patting her on her cheek. Slowly Jenny came to and looked at Todd. She grabbed his right arm and looked it over carefully.

"Oh, my gosh!" she said, "Are you alright?"

"I'm fine!" Todd assured her as he began to wiggle his fingers in front of her face. "C'mon, we gotta go."

Jenny made her way to her feet and checked herself over, too. "Okay," she said, "What do I have to do?"

"Just follow us," Todd said. "It's really cool."

Jenny closed her eyes and pushed through the wavy air behind her brother. Once inside, she continued to hold her breath. She hesitantly opened one eye and was amazed at the length of the tunnel. Her breath fizzled out of her like a leaky tire as she looked around in disbelief. Suddenly, Jenny remembered to breathe. She took a great, deep breath in and looked at Todd and began to smile. She giggled as she looked at her arms and felt the feathery sensation. "Wow, this is cool," she said. "And it smells like Grandma's sugar cookies at Christmastime!"

"Come on," Todd said, pointing at Michael. They could see him through the wavy air, asleep in his bed and unaware of their presence. "Okay, let's go."

They jumped through the window and felt the little pop as they went through. This time when they opened their eyes, they were in a classroom at Michael's school. Michael was sitting in the middle of the class desperately looking all around the room red-faced and embarrassed.

The entire classroom was full of neatly dressed students focusing very intently on the test they were taking while Michael sat in the center of the room in nothing but his underwear! He was not concentrating on his test but rather how he could possibly escape this awful place without anyone seeing him.

"Hell-ooooooo, Michael," Todd said with a great big smile, obviously enjoying his brother's predicament.

Michael turned in disbelief at the sound of his brother's voice and saw him with Jenny and Sparky just a few feet away. "No, no, no!" he said. "What the heck are you guys doing here!?"

"We came to get YOU," Todd said.

Michael took another look around the room, turning his head from one side to the other, watching as each of his classmates disappeared one by one and desk by desk until all that was left was his own darkened bedroom. He sat on the edge of his own bed, dressed in pajama bottoms and a T-shirt, much less embarrassed than a minute ago. Todd and Jenny were both giggling, waiting for Michael to speak.

"What's going on?" he said, staring at Todd with his eyes opened wide while looking around the room.

"Come on, Sparky wants to show us something," Todd said. "Oh, by the way, this is Sparky."

"No way," Michael said. "I'm just dreaming. This is a dream, right?"

"No. What you were having before was a dream, in your classroom... in your undies."

"But, we can leave and you can go back to your dream if you want," Jenny told him.

"Uh... no... I think I'll go with you guys," Michael said, bending down to look at the dog. "So, this is Sparky, huh? Can I pet him?"

"I dunno. Why don't you ask him?" Todd said.

"Does he talk?" Michael asked in all seriousness, as Todd and Jenny just looked at each other for a second, then back at Michael.

"No!" they said laughing. "He's a dog!"

"Sorry!" Michael said, looking at Sparky again. "Can I pet you?"

Sparky looked at Todd for a moment. He knew that Michael had been cruel to Todd in the past. Todd nodded. Then Sparky, who had been sitting next to Todd the whole time, looked at Michael and slowly leaned towards him so Michael could pet him.

"Okay," Todd said. "Now let's go."

Todd, Jenny and Sparky made their way toward the wavy window - the entrance to the tunnel - and showed Michael how it worked. He was leery to go in, like Jenny was at first, but once inside he was just as amazed.

"Wow!" he said. "This is the coolest thing I've ever seen!" Michael took a deep breath. "It smells just like Thanksgiving dinner!" he announced to the others.

Todd and Jenny looked at him in disbelief and said, "No, it doesn't!"

"It smells like Grandma's sugar cookies," Jenny said.

"Dad's cologne," Todd said.

Then they inhaled a deep breath through their nostrils, each trying to confirm to themselves that they were right. They did agree, however, that it smelled like home.

Again, Sparky waited patiently until they were on track to continue before he ran the length of the tunnel and jumped through the wavy window at the other end. Michael and Jenny followed after Todd.

Once they were through, they found themselves on a riverbank in the middle of winter. Sitting in about a foot and a half of snow with their legs hanging over the side of a snow bank, they could see a snowy ice-covered river.

The three Preston children stood up quickly to keep their pajamas from getting wet with snow. They soon realized, however, that the snow was not cold nor did it melt when they touched it. It was a most bizarre sensation for them to sit in the snow and to feel it scrunch underneath them. It packed like snow and tracked like snow. But when touched with their bare hands, it was not at all cold, or wet, nor did it melt like snow!

Sparky sat and watched the river while Todd, Michael, and Jenny laughed, kicked and flipped handfuls of this odd snow at one another. When Sparky let out a little "woof," they all stopped.

Off to the right from behind some trees, four boys appeared carrying rifles and dressed in warm winter clothing, with hats and gloves and boots. They were laughing and talking and making jokes as they walked along, keeping an eye on the snow-covered brush where the frozen river met the riverbank. They were hunting for rabbits.

As the Prestons watched the boys walk down the center of the river, they saw a small black and white dog running beside them.

"Hey, that's Sparky!" Todd hollered without thinking.

Now the four boys were so close, Todd could have hit them with a snowball. But when he yelled, none of them turned around—not even the Sparky on the river.

Todd cupped his hands around his mouth and hollered, "SPAR-KEY!" once more, with no response from the boys or the dog on the river. The Sparky that was sitting next to Todd, however, nudged his elbow with his nose. "I know, I know, you're right here," Todd said.

"Hey!" Michael shouted as he pointed to one of the boys. "That kid in the brown coat! That's DAD!"

"What?" Jenny said, obviously confused.

"Look! That's Dad when he was my age. Hey, Dad, ah... I mean, Thomas!" It was clear to them now that the boys could not hear them, or see them.

"Hey, wait a minute," Todd said. "I think I've been here before, but it was summertime and the boys, these boys, were swimming here, and there was a rope swing and... yeah, look, it's right there."

Todd pointed to a frozen rope lying against the backside of a leafless elm tree. All three looked at each other and then at Sparky, who was sitting intently on the bank watching the four boys on the river.

Todd, Jenny, and Michael sat down in the un-cold snow next to the little black and white dog, watching their young father and his friends hunting rabbits and talking smart.

"Hey guys, remember on Halloween when Hayden hit that car with the water balloon?" said Mike Tise, the boy at the front of the group. "And the guy stopped so fast that all he had time to do was hit his knees in the ditch, like this?"

Mike dropped down hard on his knees to demonstrate. The moment he hit the surface of the frozen water, the ice beneath him gave way. Down he went, into the freezing river and under the ice.

Without a second's hesitation, Thomas threw down his rifle and dove in after his friend.

Jenny screamed, "Dad!" But the boys couldn't hear her.

The two thrashing boys tried desperately to swim back up to the hole in the ice, but their clothes and boots were too heavy and the freezing water was too deep. The icy current was unrelenting.

Thomas was a good swimmer but not in water this cold. With its ice-like needles going right through him, and with his friend Mike trying to climb over him to get to the surface, they both panicked.

Nick Bachman and Bob Henden, the two boys in the group still on the surface, lay stretched out on their stomachs with their hands at the hole in the ice, hoping Thomas and Mike would be able to grab them.

"COME ON, HERE! RIGHT HERE!" they yelled while splashing the water.

The two boys under the ice were struck with terror, each hanging onto the other with eyes wide open, not wanting to let go and not knowing what to do, when Mike suddenly let go of Thomas' jacket and cupped his hands on each side of Thomas' face and looked him dead in the eye. Thomas stopped struggling for a second and looked at Mike who pointed downstream. Thomas understood.

The two boys on the surface were panicking and screaming at each other.

"Do something!" Bachman said to Henden.

"COME ON!" they both said yelling into the hole in the ice.

The whole time, Sparky was growling and whining, bouncing from side to side on his front paws and looking at the hole where his master had gone in.

Thomas and Mike swam downstream with the current. This was their swimming hole and they knew that just downstream were rapids. They knew the water would be shallow and the ice thinner, so they swam hard, pulling themselves along the bottom until they reached a spot where they were almost on their hands and knees. Then, with their feet planted on the bottom, they pressed with their backs against the ice, hoping to push through. On the surface, the two helpless survivors looked at each other with tear-filled eyes. Their friends were gone and there was nothing they could do! Then a terrible thought struck Bob Henden: *What am I going to tell their parents?*

Jenny, Todd, and Michael moved down by the river. With tear-filled eyes, they looked at each other in disbelief. Sparky, the boy's dog, was barking now, LOUDLY, and pawing at the ice about 30 feet from the hole in the frozen river. The Sparky that had brought the Preston children to this place, however, was sitting calmly on the riverbank.

Henden and Bachman looked downstream at Sparky, who was barking.

"I SAW THE ICE MOVE!" Bachman yelled. The two grabbed their rifles and ran downstream where Sparky was pawing the ice.

"THEY'RE HERE!" Henden screamed.

Immediately, the two boys began hammering at the ice with the butts of their rifles. As they chipped away, a two-foot piece of ice cracked and pushed up from below. With one final heave, Mike had broken through, and Thomas popped up with a powerful cough and a great breath inward, but Mike had nothing left. He lay there, motionless, face down in the frozen river.

"NOOOO!" Henden yelled.

He jumped in and broke away more chunks of ice, but now the water was only waist deep. He pulled Mike's face and chest out of the water and slid him on his back on top of the ice. Bachman was right there and pulled Mike by the shoulders of his coat, away from the hole. Then, Henden helped Thomas out of the water. He was still gasping for air and very weak. Bachman grabbed Thomas by the hand and tried to lead him to the riverbank, but Thomas wasn't about to leave Mike.

"NO! WE GOTTA HELP HIM!" Thomas screamed.

Henden looked at Thomas and said, "Roll him over!"

Thomas took hold of Mike's right arm and pulled it up and out over his head as he lay on the snow-covered ice. Henden took Mike's left elbow and put it across his chest and pushed as they rolled him over onto his stomach.

"Open his mouth," Henden ordered. "Make sure there's nothing in it."

Thomas obeyed.

Henden pushed on Mike's lower back, pressing all the way up to his shoulders. The boys watched as the water from Mike's lungs gurgled out onto the snow-covered ice, turning the fresh, powdery white snow to dark slush. Bachman looked on in sadness as the water oozed slowly through the snow in an ever-widening dark semicircle from Mike's mouth.

"Roll him over," Henden said. "Back onto his back. Yeah, that's it."

He knelt over Mike's lifeless body and pinched his nose shut with one hand and started to open his mouth, when Thomas said, "Wait. Tip his head back first to get his airway open."

"Yeah, that's right," said Henden.

They lifted Mike's neck and tipped his head back and began mouth-to-mouth resuscitation. Thomas moved around to check if Mike's heart was beating. With the ice water in his ears and Mike's wet jacket, he couldn't hear a thing.

"Come on, BREATHE!" Bachman said over and over. "Breathe!"

Henden blew into Mike's mouth for about the fifteenth time. Getting light-headed, he turned to Thomas. "Can you take over?" he asked him.

Just then, Mike coughed hard, his face scrunching in pain. He coughed again and again until he began to breathe on his own. Thomas and Mike looked at each other in silence. They didn't need to say anything. It was all there, in both their eyes.

"Thanks for saving my life," Mike said.

"Let's get out of here," Bachman said. "We gotta get out of these wet clothes—NOW!"

Bachman and Henden helped their friends off the river.

"I would never have thought to go downstream," Thomas said to Mike. "That's what saved us."

"Well, I could never have broken through the ice by myself, either. I knew when you came in after me, you weren't gonna quit on me, so I wasn't gonna quit on you either!"

"I guess we saved each other," Thomas replied.

The four boys agreed that they would never tell anyone about the accident for fear that one of their parents might find out, and they wouldn't be allowed to go hunting together again.

Todd, Jenny, and Michael were still speechless at the events they had just witnessed, when Sparky let out one little "woof." They all turned to look at him. The little black dog was just sitting in the snow wagging his tail. Next to him they saw the wavy air again in a window-like shape.

Sparky stood up and jumped through the wavy window.

"Let's go," said Todd.

Jenny and Michael just shrugged and followed Todd through the wavy air into the tunnel where Sparky was waiting for them. Once they were all inside, the little dog ran the length of the tunnel and jumped out the other side. With a good running start, the Prestons followed him. When they emerged on the other side, they were standing at the steps of a small house that was under construction.

"Hey! I know this place! It's the cabin I told you guys about in one of my first dreams," Todd said, noticing that now most of the stud walls were up and the smell of fresh cut lumber filled the air.

Sparky walked right up the front steps and lay down on the floor, chewing on a small block of wood that had been left by the builders. Michael sat down on a sawhorse and looked around.

"Well, what now?" he said to no one in particular.

No sooner had the words come out of Michael's mouth, when he saw an old, light-blue pickup truck pull into the driveway. He heard two doors slam and saw two men walking toward the steps carrying tools. A moment's panic set in. They didn't think they were supposed to be there. Then the smallest one came up the steps, and there he was again... Thomas... their father... this time, about 15 years old. Grandpa Rich was with him. He looked only about 40 years old.

Last up the steps came Sparky, Thomas' dog. He walked right over to the same corner where Todd's Sparky was laying down and started chewing on a small block of wood. It looked very strange to the three siblings to see both Sparkys, side by side, chewing similar blocks of wood at the same time. But once again, as before, Thomas and Rich had no clue the kids were there.

Todd spoke first. He and Jenny had tiptoed over to Michael on the sawhorse and began to whisper just in case he might be heard. "See you guys? Remember the dream I told you about at breakfast the other day? This is the place. Only I wasn't this close before. And I didn't know the boy I saw was Dad. Or that this was Grandpa Rich."

"Yeah. OK. I remember," said Michael. "You're the dream king—"

Their whispers were interrupted.

"Hey, buddy," Grandpa Rich said to young Thomas. "Grab the rest of those nails we bought from out of the truck. And bring me the level and the chalk line. I want to get this bathroom wall up before your mom gets here with our lunch."

"Okay, Dad," young Thomas said as he ran across the floor, jumping all three steps just like he had done in Todd's dream.

They watched him open the door to the truck. Todd remembered Grandpa Rich's story about Sparky getting sprayed by the skunk.

"Hey! That's the truck with the camper top that they used to sleep in... the one they were in when Sparky got sprayed by the skunk."

Todd's Sparky looked up from his block of wood as if he understood the word skunk. He looked at Todd and cocked his head.

"No, no, Sparky. No skunk."

Michael touched Todd with one hand and Jenny with the other and said, "I don't understand why we're here. Are we just supposed to sit here and watch them build a whole cabin?"

"I don't know," Todd said as they watched, enjoying what they were seeing.

Though Rich and Thomas were working, they were having fun, too. They were just talking about the job at hand. Even the kids could see how much Rich enjoyed teaching Thomas how to build. Thomas was eager to show his dad that he understood the process and knew what needed to be done next. Rich was happy to encourage this, too. He would say, "Okay, now what do we need for tools?" or "Thomas, what do we need to do before we set this wall into place?" When he was right, Rich would say,

"Atta boy... now you're getting it." If he was wrong, Rich would say, "Yes, but we need one more thing as well," or "That's true, we need to do that, but we need to do what else first?"

They had fun with each other, too. Rich was holding the ladder while Thomas measured from the top plate of the bathroom wall to a mark on one of the rafters. Thomas kept tapping the brim of Rich's cap with the toe of one foot as he stretched to reach the mark. He did this at least three times without Rich catching on. The fourth time, he gave it a downward swat, knocking Rich's cap over his eyes. Thomas couldn't hold back any longer. He burst out laughing loudly.

"You little squirt!" Rich said. "Were you doing that on purpose the whole time?"

Thomas, who was laughing harder than ever now, just nodded and held his stomach as he laughed. The three Preston children were laughing hard as well. They were all very comfortable watching their father and Grandpa Rich from years gone by. They were all very happy to be part of the Preston family. They could hear the joy, feel the love, and sense the pride in that small, unfinished room.

Then, out of the blue, Thomas asked, "Dad, am I a man yet?"

Rich put down his level and looked at Thomas and smiled. They sat cross-legged on the floor facing each other.

"Well, buddy, right now you are more of a man than an awful lot of grown-up males I know. You give me a good day's work, you don't complain too much, you take responsibility for your mistakes, you're respectful to me, and you're willing to do what it takes to make a better place for this family. So, in those ways, you are very much a man."

"So, how will I know when I'm all the way there?" Thomas asked him.

"Well, that's a good question," Rich said. "In some places, a boy must go through a rite of passage to be considered a man, like hunting a lion or something. In other cultures, when you turn a certain age they have a ceremony for you. After that, you are given more grown-up responsibilities and you are considered a man."

"What do you say is the best way to know?"

Rich smiled again and said, "If you're old enough to ask, then you're old enough to hear it. The best thing I can tell you is something that was told to me when I was about your age by your favorite uncle, Uncle Doug, who was a wise old fellow. He was kind of grumpy and all business. We all called him Captain. He always wanted to see what we knew about life and teach us lessons and so on. So, he would ask us questions about all sorts of things, like fishing, sailing, current events, or whatever. Then, he would just sit back and listen, usually with a big smirk on his face. I didn't know it at the time, but he was trying to find out if we were going to pretend we knew more about a topic then we did. If he thought we were full of hot air, as he called it, he would ask more detailed questions until we'd have to admit we weren't really sure about our previous answer."

Rich began telling Thomas about the time he and his dad went on a camping and fishing trip, and how they sat around the campfire listening to Uncle Doug after the work was done for the day.

"It was Dad and me, with Dad's friend and his son, and Uncle Doug." Rich said. "Uncle Doug started talking about this very subject. So now, I'll tell you as closely as I remember it. He said: *Boys, I'm gonna tell you somethin' now and I want you to pay attention, copy?* That was the Captain's way of asking us boys if we understood. And when he said that, we were to say *Copy, Captain.* That way, he knew that we'd heard him and understood his instructions. I don't remember it word for word, but I never forgot the gist of what he said that day."

"What did he say?" young Thomas asked anxiously.

"He said: *Boys, you're coming up on a time in your life that is very important. There's gonna be things that you will be allowed to do and some things that you will be able to choose to do, or not to do. For example, soon*

102

*you will be able to drive a car, and that's great fun, and motorcycles too...
lots of fun. But, with that fun comes responsibility. You need to choose
them wisely. Not long after that, you'll be able to drink liquor and smoke
cigarettes, if you choose, and that's up to you. I'm not gonna sit here and say
you can't do any of it cause you've seen me on this trip smoking more than
one cigarette. That's my habit and I don't like it, but it's mine! You have to
choose. I wish I'd had someone tell me not to smoke before I ever got started.
I wouldn't be stuck on them now. So, that being said, I'm telling you now,
don't start! Copy?* We'd automatically respond and say *Copy, Captain!"*

Rich continued to tell Thomas more about what Uncle Doug said to
them that night around the campfire.

"Uncle Doug went on, saying: *You boys are young and full of life. You
wanna kick up your heels now and again, and I get that. There's nothing
wrong with that. But one thing you may or may not know yet is that life is
a precious thing, and it can be taken away in one second of carelessness. So,
when you're out in your cars running around chasing girls, leave the liquor*

*at home. That goes for any of them other funny drugs they got out there nowadays, too. I want you to remember this: these people that want to sell you that crap—drugs, I mean. They don't care if you live or die. Understand? They just don't care! All they want is to get you hooked on their stuff and take your money. Now, the reason I'm telling you this is because I've known too many young men just like you. They were good boys, but they made one bad decision and it cost them their lives, or others' lives, or they hurt someone else they cared about, and now they'll never be the same because of some careless decision. How would you feel if someone you loved was hurt bad 'cause of you? Don't do that to yourselves, and don't do it to your parents. You've never seen such pain as a parent who's had to bury a child, and I hope you never do. I want you all to have the chance to grow up and become good men, to meet a beautiful girl and fall in love, maybe raise a family of your own someday. These are fine and wonderful things, but you can't do any of them if you're careless or if you allow other people to manipulate you into doing things you know you shouldn't do. Copy?* And, we all said *Copy, Captain.*"

Rich paused, then continued. "Uncle Doug had a lot to say. He told us that it was incumbent upon us to decide what kind of men we were going to be. *He said: And hear this... there is nothing more important than family. Be men of honor, not cowards. The world's got plenty of cowards and I've seen it all... too much of it... in school, in business, in government and in the church. There's too many of 'em. If you do something wrong, own up to it, be a man and take the consequences. So, you boys be men of honor, and fall in love and raise good children who will do the same. I'm sorry to say, that I see this country going down a dangerous path and you boys, you and your friends, and your generation are what we are going to need to straighten it out, alright? Do you copy?* We all answered, *Copy, Captain!* clearly and quickly. We could tell he was getting a little wound up, and nobody wanted to make him any more upset. Then he said: *Good. Now,*

*I'm sorry for talking so bluntly, but it's something I believe in very strongly. And I believe you need to hear it plain. Now, that's all I have to say on the subject. Let's get back to having fun.* And we did!"

"Wow," Thomas said. "That was quite a speech!"

"Yes, it was," Rich said. "It sure left an impression on me, I can tell you that! So, now I've told you, and someday you can tell your sons or daughters—girls need to hear it, too. I think what Captain Doug had to say applies to everyone."

Rich paused. "Thomas, I want you to think about what I just told you because Uncle Doug's words are just as true today as ever. Don't be a coward, and remember, you only have one life to live, so live it well! Make good choices, alright?"

"Did you ever come up with your own code of honor, Dad?" Thomas wanted to know.

Rich smiled a great big smile and said, "Well, as a matter of fact, I did. Would you like to hear it?"

"Sure," Thomas said.

"Let me just start by saying that when Captain Doug first gave us that speech, I thought about it often. I thought about people I knew, people I wanted to be like, and what I came up with was this: I believe in the Golden Rule—do unto others as you would have them do unto you. I believe that if you must choose a course of action that will have a negative result, you should choose the path which will cause the least pain, whether that pain is physical or emotional. The only time you may choose a path of more pain is when that pain is your own, like giving up something you really want for a friend. That's pretty much my code of honor in a nutshell, Thomas, but I would like you to come up with some ideas of your own, and maybe we can talk about this again in a month or two."

Thomas nodded.

"Oh, and one more thing. It's not just our talents that make us who we are. It is the choices we make when things get tough. Those choices show who we truly are. Wouldn't it be nice if we were at our best all the time?"

With that, the three Preston children looked at each other with eyebrows raised and said, "Wow, I guess that's what Sparky brought us here for!"

Thomas' Sparky was asleep in the sun on the unfinished living room floor. Todd's Sparky was at the bottom of the steps ready to go. As the children made their way towards him, they saw the familiar wavy window of air but waited for Sparky to lead the way.

Jumping into the tunnel first, then waiting until everyone was inside, Sparky ran through the tunnel out the other side. The Prestons followed.

When they jumped out at the opposite end, they were surprised to find themselves sitting in the back seat of their mother's car driving down State Street on a dark and rainy night.

"Mom!" Jenny yelled without thinking. "I know, I know, she can't hear me."

"Look, she's crying," said Todd.

Michael and Jenny leaned over the back seat to see for themselves. Mary Ann rarely ever cried, just at sad movies or at weddings but not in real life, and they could see she was crying pretty hard, too.

"What's wrong? What could it be? Why is she crying?" they asked one another.

"Hey! Yellow light! Mom! Stop!" Michael yelled. "The light's changing, Mom!"

Without warning, they heard the blaring horn of a pickup truck and saw it pass by, inches from the front of their car. They felt the car skid out of control and slide all the way around to face oncoming traffic.

"Ahhh!" Todd hollered.

"Mom! Mom! Get off the road," Michael kept yelling.

Mary Ann grabbed the gearshift, jammed it into reverse and hit the

gas. They heard the whirring tires and watched as traffic headed straight towards them while they slowly climbed up the curb and onto the sidewalk.

"WHOA! Did that really happen?" Michael yelled. "Did we just see something that happened to our mom, or is this something that's going to happen? Sparky, why did you bring us here!"

Sparky's ears and head went down, and he looked very ashamed of himself. Jenny tried to console her mother, still forgetting she could not be seen or heard.

The children were all aware of the onlookers staring at their mother as she made her way off the sidewalk to the abandoned parking lot. They had never felt so sad as they did right then, to sit there so utterly helpless, watching their mother sobbing, knowing there was nothing they could do for her.

Once again, the wavy air appeared and they reluctantly went through it. Michael gave Sparky a look of extreme anger as he pointed his finger at the little black dog.

"This better be the last time you show us anything like that! DO YOU UNDERSTAND ME?" Michael said.

Sparky bowed his head, then looked up slowly at Michael, offering him his paw to shake. "Yeah, yeah, whatever, you little dirt bag, you heard me."

Sparky didn't move except to lower his head a bit more and lift his paw a little higher until Michael finally shook hands with him. "Well, alright then, let's go."

One by one, the Preston children climbed through the wavy window of air and into the tunnel. They made their way to the other end and jumped through. Now, all three were at home in their separate beds. It was 12:32 a.m. on Friday morning.

Michael had only been in bed for about two hours. *Wow,* he thought. *All that happened in two hours' time? How in the world?* He was stunned. He thought about his mother and bolted out of bed, heading for her bedroom. In the hallway, he ran right into his brother and sister, who apparently had the same idea.

"I wanna see if Mom's alright," Todd said.

"Me, too," Jenny replied.

The three children tiptoed to her bedroom door and ever so carefully turned the knob to peek inside. Their mother was fine, laying there on her back, mouth open and snoring peacefully.

Todd and Jenny backed away from the door as Michael slowly closed it. Releasing the knob, Michael motioned for Jenny and Todd to follow him into his room, the farthest away from Mary Ann's bedroom and the safest place to talk.

The three climbed on top of Michael's bed, and in a voice as calm and as even-toned as he could muster, Michael began to talk.

"Have either of you had any dreams or had anything interesting happen to you tonight?"

Todd and Jenny looked at each other dumbfounded for a moment, and then both said, "YEAH!"

"What are you talkin' about, Michael?" Todd asked. "You were with us the whole time!"

Jenny nodded in agreement.

"The boys on the ice... Dad falling through... Grandpa and Dad at the cabin... MOM IN THE CAR!" Todd said.

"Whew. Okay. Okay. I thought maybe it was just my dream," Michael said.

The Preston children recounted many of the scenes they had witnessed in their dream adventures and wondered what it all meant. They discussed the dreams until almost 2 a.m. before Michael suggested they continue talking in the morning.

"We'd better get back to bed or we'll fall asleep in school tomorrow."

They all agreed to meet back in Michael's room after school, before their mom got home that afternoon.

# 9

In school the next day, Michael replayed the adventures of the night before in his mind. He made notes in his journal about questions he had and things he wanted to discuss with his brother and sister.

Jenny, however, wanted desperately to talk to her friends about what had happened, but she didn't know how to bring it up. When she finally decided to talk to Megan - her oldest and most trusted friend - Megan wasn't feeling very friendly. Ever since Jenny decided she wanted to be one of the cool girls and be *in* with Amber Jackson and the group of *in* girls, Jenny had been snubbing her and treating her like she was second class. Megan was also still very angry with Jenny over the shoplifting incident at the mall, where Jenny had decided for both of them to steal for Amber and her friends.

"Well... look who's decided to lower herself and come visit with us commoners," Megan said to Jenny in front of some friends.

Jenny knew instantly that she had it coming and deserved anything else that Megan wanted to dish out. She knew she had been a terrible friend, and it was all because Amber Jackson had not thought Megan was *with it* enough for the cool girls. Now Jenny was the one feeling terrible. All she wanted to do was apologize.

"Megan, please, I implore you," Jenny said in a most sincere way. "Can I talk to you in private? It's about my mom."

Megan realized that whatever it was, it must be very important to Jenny. She looked around at her other friends, then back at Jenny and said flatly, "No, you made your choice. You chose Amber, so that's that. You could have gotten me in some serious trouble with that little favor you did for her, and you didn't even talk to me about it first. You just assumed I'd go along with you. And ever since, I've been feeling awful about it. So, whatever your little problem is, I don't want to hear it! Go tell it to your new best friend, Amber. I'm sure she'd love to help you out," Megan said to the other girls, turning on her heels. "Come on. Let's go." And they all walked away from Jenny Preston, who knew Megan was right.

Jenny felt awful about the theft as well, so she knew Megan must feel exactly the same way. She also knew she had to make it up to Megan somehow, and an apology wasn't going to be enough. It would have to be something big. So, for the next few days, Jenny tried to talk to Megan, but Megan was not interested.

Finally, at the end of the third day, Jenny cornered Megan by her locker when none of the other girls were around. "I know you don't want to talk to me," she said.

Megan was silent.

"That's fine," Jenny continued. "But just listen to me for one minute, and then I'll leave you alone."

"Fine," Megan said. "What is it?"

"I know you're hurting, and I know it's my fault."

"Okay... go on," Megan said.

"I'm sorry... I'm sorry for the way I acted... and I'm sorry I got mixed up with Amber, and... I'm sorry I put you in a situation that could have gotten you into so much trouble."

"You're SORRY? That's IT? Well, that's just NOT gonna cut it, sister!"

"I know," Jenny said. "That's why I've decided to take it all back. I promise, I won't mention your name or anyone else's. I'll just take it all back to the stores and tell them I did it, that I felt bad about it. So, feel free to call my parents, or the police, or whoever you have to call to get this over with."

Megan was shocked. "Do you really mean that? I thought you gave all that stuff to Amber."

"No, I was going to, but a security guy and his buddy were standing around the food court when I was trying to give it to her, so she told me to keep it and just bring it to school."

"So, hasn't Amber been after you to bring it to school?" Megan asked, genuinely surprised..

"Yeah, she certainly has," Jenny told her.

"Well, what have you been telling her?"

"The first day, I just told her that I forgot it. The second day, I told her that my mom was all over me about something else, so I couldn't grab it."

Megan smiled. "And today, what have you told her today?"

"I haven't told her anything. I've been avoiding her all day."

Megan's smile widened. She was clearly enjoying Jenny's misery.

"Alright," Megan said. "I'll think about it tonight and let you know tomorrow. But, don't do anything with that stuff until I talk to you tomorrow."

"Okay, I won't. But what are you going to think about?" Jenny asked.

"I'm going to think about whether I believe you or not, and if you're sincere or not. Then, I'll decide if I'm going to help you with the problem with your mom, or not," Megan added. She really wanted Jenny to have to suffer a little more before she helped her.

The next day came slowly. All Jenny wanted to do was find Megan to see if she was going to have her friend back, and to stay away from Amber Jackson. But it wasn't until after lunchtime that Jenny finally caught up with Megan, who had always liked Jenny's mom and was secretly dying to know what had Jenny in such a state about her mother. So, when the two finally met in the library, Megan sighed and said, "Oh, alright, tell me what's up with your mom and I'll see what I can do."

The girls went off and found a suitable spot to talk. Jenny started by saying, "I had a dream." She didn't get into all the details, focusing only on her mom and the car accident while Megan listened, wide-eyed. Jenny recounted in vivid detail her mother's car accident.

"Yeah, but it was just a dream, right?" Megan asked.

"I don't know. I don't think so. I feel like my mom's in terrible trouble. I'm not sure if this accident was something that happened, or if it was a premonition. Either way, I don't know how to help her, but I do know it was more than just a dream. I can tell you that for sure."

Megan was surprisingly sympathetic and tried to put Jenny's mind at ease the best she could. The two sat in silence for several moments.

"Well, you don't know if she was in an accident," Megan finally responded. "And even if she's going to be, you said you were with her in the dream through the whole thing and she didn't get hurt, right? AND, nobody else got hurt either, right?"

Jenny's eyes brightened. "Hey, that's right... but in the dream she was really crying hard, and I've never seen my mom cry." Jenny held back about all the other things she'd seen in the dream because it would have been too much to share with Megan all at once. Nevertheless, it seemed as though Megan was back as Jenny's good friend.

*******

Todd thought about the dream off and on over the next few days. But, he knew in his heart that Sparky was here for something good. Though he didn't know how to explain it, he just knew that his family would be better off if they paid attention to what this little black dog was trying to show them.

*******

The first one home the following afternoon was Michael, who skipped out of study hall—the last period of the day—to jog home. After he ran his backpack up to his room, he returned downstairs to begin picking up the family room. He picked up clothes and put them in a pile for laundering. He picked up snack wrappers and dishes and brought them to the kitchen. He was zooming around, trying to get as much done as possible before his mother came home.

Todd came home next. When he walked in, he saw Michael vacuuming the family room. Michael didn't see Todd, who snuck across the entryway and into the kitchen where he could watch Michael without being seen. Todd smiled. Michael never vacuumed without being told, and he was enjoying watching his brother work.

As the vacuum whirred slowly down to a stop, Michael began winding up the cord when Todd said quite loudly, "YOU MISSED A SPOT!"

Michael just about jumped out of his skin. "AUHH! You scared the crap out of me!"

Todd was quite pleased with himself. "What are you doing?" he asked with sincerity.

"Cleaning," Michael said, "And you're going to help me."

"No, I'm not."

"Yes, you are. And Jen's going to help us, too, when she gets home."

"Why?"

"Because something's going on with Mom... she's upset or something, and I don't want her to have any reason to be upset with us."

"Good idea," Todd said. "What can I do?"

"Grab that wastebasket from the kitchen. Put that stuff in it." Then, he motioned to the trash he had piled up. "And take it out to the curb."

"Okay," Todd said.

Michael looked startled watching his brother do what he was told without an argument. And when Jenny walked in, she just stood there with her mouth open while her two brothers focused on their cleaning tasks.

Todd looked at Jenny as he passed her on the way to taking out the garbage. "We're cleaning," he said.

"Yes, I can see that," Jenny replied. "Why?"

"We just wanna make it nice for Mom."

Jenny put her books down and jumped right in to help. She ran some soap and water into the sink and started doing the last of the dishes from breakfast after wiping off the kitchen counter. They had the house in pretty good shape when Mary Ann walked in the door.

"Hi, Mom," they all said at once.

"Wow! The place looks great!" she said. "Did you guys do all this by yourselves without being told? That's wonderful. What's the occasion?"

"We, ah... we just wanted it nice for you and Dad, for when he gets home tonight," Jenny said.

"Well, that's very nice, very thoughtful of you guys. Thank you."

Todd and Jenny smiled at each other. They were proud of what they had done. Michael, who wanted to know if Mary Ann had actually been in the car accident they'd seen in their dream, had an idea but couldn't just ask her straight out. He got right down to business and started laying the groundwork for his plan.

"Mom... we were in Driver's Ed today and they showed a film about car accidents."

Mary Ann froze for a second. She put down her purse and hung up her coat. She made no obvious sign that this was a bad topic.

"Yes, what about them?" she asked. "Did you learn how not to get in one?" she said in a bright voice with her back turned toward him.

"Well, they talked about insurance, police reports, damage reports and things like that and—"

Just then, the phone rang. It was Thomas.

"Hi, honey," Mary Ann said brightly. "The kids got the house all cleaned up and ready for you and—What? WHAT? Oh, Thomas, you're not serious!"

All three of the Preston children were listening to Mary Ann and knew something was wrong. They listened intently to see if they could catch the meaning from their mother's half of the conversation.

"Thomas, what am I supposed to tell the kids? Well... well... I just can't believe you're doing this! Everyone was looking forward to you coming home, and I have something important I need to talk to you about. I've been waiting to tell you, to explain, and I... I... no, I just can't do it over the phone! Thomas, I'm so upset with you right now I can't even think straight! Well, when? When WILL you be home? That's fine, Thomas. Whatever YOU want—as usual."

Mary Ann hung up the phone hard and turned around with a look of anger and frustration on her face. Michael, Jenny and Todd stared at their mother with a mixture of sadness, apprehension and disappointment in their eyes.

"Anything we can do?" Michael said hopefully.

"No," Mary Ann said. "You all heard it. Your father's not coming home tonight like we thought. Your father said he'd be home in a few days. There was something at work that was unavoidable and very important. He asked me to apologize to all of you, and he hopes you'll understand that this one just couldn't be helped. Now, let's get some supper started, shall we?"

Jenny knew that when the subject was changed, she should not push her mother any further. Mary Ann moved toward the kitchen and kept her back to her children so they couldn't see her face.

"What did you need to tell him, Mom," Jenny asked. "You know, the important thing?"

Mary Ann discretely wiped her eyes on the back of her sleeve and tried to smile before she turned around. "Oh, nothing, honey... not to worry," she said to Jenny as she milled around the kitchen, checking cupboards and so on to get herself together without the children seeing her this upset and hurt. "That's just something between your father and me."

Deciding against upsetting his mother further, Michael began hinting his way around to find out about the accident, and while Mary Ann was on the phone he had a thought. Remembering he had mentioned police reports and damage reports when he was telling her about the imaginary conversation from Driver's Ed, he got an idea.

"I'm going to put my bike in the garage," he said as he stood up. "I'll be right back."

Michael ran to the garage, grabbed the flashlight from the workbench and began inspecting the driver's side of the car. He not only found small marks on both wheels from where the car slid into the curb but also scrapes on the side of the rear tire, which must have been made when Mary Ann hit the gas and spun the tires up the curb and onto the sidewalk. He was pleased with himself and his discovery. He now knew for certain the accident was real and that it had already happened.

Michael put the flashlight away and went back into the house, where Todd was busy helping out by setting the table. He caught Jenny on her way down the stairs before she got too close to the kitchen, and began to explain to her what he'd found out.

"Huh?" Jenny gasped and looked wide-eyed at Michael. "That means she really was in an accident!" she exclaimed.

"Shhhh... we'll have to tell Todd after supper," Michael said, with Jenny nodding in agreement.

Not long after, they finished supper and were clearing the table when the doorbell rang. Grandpa Rich pushed the door open and stuck his head inside without waiting for anyone to answer it.

"Anybody home?" he called out.

"Grandpa!" Todd hollered and ran to the door.

Grandpa Rich and Grandma Karen came inside and said their hellos to everyone. "I hope this isn't a bad time," Karen said.

"Of course not," Mary Ann said graciously. "Come on in the living room and have a seat. Would you like some coffee?"

"Yes, that would be wonderful," Karen replied.

"I suppose you've heard that Thomas isn't coming home tonight" said Mary Ann.

"Yes. That's one of the reasons we're here," Rich said. "That, and to see you. We also wanted to see how big these grandkids are getting, of course," he said as he tousled Todd's hair. "I tell you what, Mary Ann, I don't know, but I think you're just about a saint the way you put up with that son of mine."

The phone rang. "Hold that thought," Mary Ann said as she went to answer it.

It was Reggie. They hadn't spoken since the night of their dinner—and the kiss.

"Is this a good time?" Reggie asked. "Can we talk?"

"No. No, not really," Mary Ann said calmly into the phone as she smiled at her in-laws sitting just a few feet away.

"Please, Mary Ann. I've been hoping to talk to you for a week now, but you haven't been in," Reggie continued.

"Okay, just a minute." Mary Ann put her hand over the receiver, told her in-laws she had to take this call and that it would just be a minute. Then she stepped into another room.

"Well, I'll get the coffee started," Karen said. "I know my way around your kitchen."

Karen proceeded to get the coffee and filters and began filling up the pot with water for the coffee, when she overheard Mary Ann in the other room.

"No, Reggie. I can't... I can't talk right now. No. No, I know it won't happen again. We just can't do that. We can talk about it tomorrow. Yes, I'll call you."

When Mary Ann came around the corner to the kitchen, she was startled to see Karen already there. "Just getting the coffee started for you, hun," she said with a sweet smile.

Mary Ann's stomach sank. *Oh, my God,* she thought. *Please tell me Karen didn't hear any of that.* The two women smiled, made small talk and politely waited for the coffee to brew before joining the others in the living room.

"Oh, that's smells wonderful!" Rich said and abruptly adding, "I want to apologize for Thomas."

"It's not your fault, Rich. You don't have anything to apologize for," Mary Ann said.

"But I've seen this getting worse the last few months. I've spoken to Thomas about it and it just doesn't seem to do any good," he continued.

"What exactly have you seen, Rich?" Mary Ann asked.

"Oh, that he's spending more and more time away from home. That his work and his goal and his career path seem to be the only things that are important to him anymore, you know? He would say, 'Gotta get ahead of the game.' Or, 'Just a little more time and I'll have it all set.' Or, 'Do you want me to quit?' He's always saying things like that."

"I know, Rich, I've heard him say all those things for a long time now, but really, you don't have anything to apologize for," Mary Ann said.

"Well, I guess not, but the last time I took him to the airport I gave him some things to think about, and I hope he did. I hope it may have done some good, and I wish I would have told him sooner."

"What did you say to him?" Mary Ann asked.

"Well, I asked him if he was happy, for one thing." Rich said. "Then, I asked him to honestly think about two things: One, if he enjoyed his work, and two, how would he know when it was enough... when he was a success in his own mind."

"What did he say?"

"Well, basically, he promised he'd think about it," Rich replied.

Karen was very quiet as Rich and Mary Ann talked, but her imagination was in overdrive. She kept thinking about what she had overheard when Mary Ann was on the phone.

*Who is this Reggie?*

*What won't happen again?*

*And what is it they just couldn't do?*

Oh, she could hardly stand it. She just wanted to finish that coffee and get in the car and talk with Rich about it. Then her mind would start again.

*What kind of person is this Reggie?*

*Where does he work?*

*How can I find out for sure what's going on?*

Then Mary Ann spoke, and Karen snapped back into the conversation at hand.

"I don't know," Mary Ann said to her in-laws. "I just feel like something's missing, and I've felt this way for a long time... months now. I feel like there's a hole in my life, and I'm trying to fill it with work, volunteering at the museum and doing things for the kids' schools. But, I just have this empty feeling inside that I can't put my finger on, you understand?"

Rich nodded sympathetically. "Well, you know we love you, Mary Ann, as if you were our own daughter. If you think of anything that we can do to help, just let us know."

"Thanks, Rich. That means a lot."

When they finished their coffee and conversation, Grandpa Rich and Grandma Karen headed for home. Karen was still thinking about what she had overheard but decided not to say anything to Rich, especially after his words about loving Mary Ann like their own daughter. Yet, she couldn't just sit back and do nothing. She thought about it over and over in her mind that night and couldn't think of a good way to interpret what she had overheard.

Whatever was going on here, it directly affected her son. She would tell him what she heard and let him figure out what to make of it.

*******

That morning after Rich left to run an errand, Karen called Thomas on his cell phone. She explained the situation, how she came to be in the kitchen when Mary Ann was on the phone, and how she overheard his wife talking to a man.

"I didn't hear much, Thomas," Karen said to her son. "But what I did hear was Mary Ann saying *no* to Reggie, and that she couldn't talk at the moment. She also told him it won't happen again, and... something about how they just can't do that—whatever *that* is."

To Karen's credit, what she told Thomas was true, word for word, but she was a worried mother looking out for her son. So, when she told it to Thomas, he understood it exactly as she had worried about it.

"Thomas," she said, "There's something else, too. Mary Ann said she felt like there was a hole in her life somehow, and she was trying to fill it."

Thomas' heart sank. He felt like he had been hit in the stomach, full force with a baseball bat.

"Thomas, I just don't know what to make of it. I hope it's nothing, but I thought you should know," Karen said.

*Wow... I didn't see this coming, Thomas thought. I knew Mary Ann wanted me home more, but never thought for a second that she might be seeing someone else.*

*Had my father been right?* he questioned.

*Did I put my career first for so long that I am now losing my wife and my family?*

Thomas collapsed on the bed.

"Ah... thanks, Mom," he finally said to Karen. "I'll be home tomorrow night about 7:15."

He lay on his back staring up at the ceiling with the ache in his stomach growing stronger and stronger, his eyes pooling with tears.

# 10

The next day, Thomas did nothing but finish up his business as quickly as possible at his company's home office. He thought about his family. All he wanted to do was to get back home. So, he managed to catch an earlier flight, all the while going over in his mind what he would say to Mary Ann.

After the plane landed, he quickly grabbed his bags and got a cab without letting anyone know he would be home early. When he arrived, he paid the cab driver and retrieved his bags from the trunk. The house looked deserted from the front walk. Bikes and baseball gear lay unattended on the front lawn. Thomas thought it looked absolutely wonderful. He walked in the front door, put his bags and briefcase down and hollered, "Hey, anybody home?"

Mary Ann had just come in the back door carrying an empty flowerpot and wearing gardening gloves. Her long hair was in a ponytail, sticking out of the back of baseball cap. With smudged dirt on her face and in an old college sweatshirt, Thomas told her she looked beautiful.

"Oh, yeah. Whatever. I look a mess," she said. "And... by the way, mister, what are you doing home so early? I wasn't expecting you until 7:15 or so."

"Yeah, I got an earlier flight," Thomas responded.

"You should have called, ya know," Mary Ann said with a stern look.

"I just wanted to get back here and see everyone as soon as I could. Look, I really missed you, and I just wanted to tell you I'm sorry. I'm sorry, I've been gone so much, and I'm sorry I haven't been around here to help with the house and the kids. I wanted to tell you about what's been going on at work and why I wasn't able to explain before, you know, on the phone last night about what was happening," Thomas said, fumbling with his words.

"Listen Thomas, I know your work is very important to you... probably the most important. I've given up trying to get you to stay home, to do more, or whatever. But something happened this time while you were gone, and I really need to talk to you about it," Mary Ann explained.

She had been dreading this conversation for over a week, and now that the time was here, she just felt sick to her stomach and didn't know how to start. She looked down at the floor.

"It has to do with lots of things," she began, "but mostly with my work at the museum and with Reggie. You know, Reggie, my friend who I always talk with about my art stuff and art history, right?"

"Yes, I know who you mean."

Now, Thomas felt sick, too. He felt as if he'd taken a kick in the stomach again, similar to the feeling that he'd had after speaking to Karen, but this was worse. Now, it was coming from his wife. He just knew Mary Ann was going to tell him she wanted a divorce.

Mary Ann continued telling Thomas about working at the museum, like they often did, no big deal, and doing good work on the art show project and getting lots of things decided.

Thomas' mind was racing. *What should I do?* he thought. *Can't I stop this somehow? Am I just supposed to sit here and listen to this?*

"Well, we were getting hungry and Reggie said he would go and get a couple of Cokes and some granola bars for us, you know," Mary Ann continued. "He was gone a long time. Then, something smelled really good and he said, 'Dinner is served,' and when I went into the Danforth Parlor, he had Peking Duck for us... and wine... and it was really good... and the room was so beautiful. I... I just felt like royalty, or a celebrity from back in the 20s, you know, and then—"

"DADDY!" Todd yelled, interrupting as he came running at Thomas from the back door, arms wide and smiling. Thomas bent down on one knee and scooped up his son with both arms and spun him around and kissed him on the cheek.

"Dad! You'll never guess what happened!" Todd exclaimed.

"Ah... you missed me so much you couldn't eat dessert for a whole week?"

"Nooooo!" Todd replied. "I had some more dreams about Sparky. Michael and Jenny had 'em too, and he showed us stuff, stuff about you and Grandpa when you were a boy, and ah..." Todd had run out of breath.

Michael and Jenny came through the front door, and each gave their father a hug and said hello. Todd had started in again trying to explain more about the dreams.

"And... I saw Michael at school in one of them, and he told me that was exactly what had happened two days before. Then, I had a dream about Jenny and Megan, and Amber Jackson." Todd made a face, letting everyone know that he did not like Amber Jackson.

Thomas wasn't hearing much of what his youngest son was trying so hard to explain to him. He was hugging Michael and Jenny as they were saying their hellos, and looking desperately at Mary Ann, trying to detect the slightest clue as to what was coming next, still nodding politely to

Todd, as if he were listening. He kept looking at Mary Ann, hoping to lock eyes with her, let her know somehow that he still loved her and wanted to finish their conversation.

In an effort to help her little brother, Jenny said, "Dad, you really do need to hear about the dreams Todd's been explaining to you."

"Knock, knock," came a voice from the front door. "Oh, by gosh, Thomas, you're here!" exclaimed Grandpa Rich. "Hey Karen! Karen, he's already here! Come on in!" Rich hollered over his shoulder. "When did you get home and why didn't you let anyone know, Thomas?"

*Because... I wanted to have... well... I wanted to have an important and private conversation with my wife,* Thomas thought but did not say. "I just wanted to surprise Mary Ann."

Grandma Karen came through the door, and both grandparents made their way to the living room to sit down.

"So, when did you get back?" Rich asked again.

"Oh, I've only been home about two minutes," Thomas replied.

Mary Ann told the children to put their school bags and notebooks upstairs in their rooms and come back down to talk to their grandparents for a little while. Then, she went to the kitchen to get some drinks for everyone.

"Well, we just hadn't seen you in a while and thought we'd stop over for a visit and make sure everything's alright," Rich said.

"What do you mean? Alright?" Thomas asked.

"Oh, you know, you've been gone an awful lot lately. Just wanted to see how it's going. Have you thought anymore about what I asked you to think about on our way to the airport?"

"Yes, Dad. I have. I've thought about it quite a bit on this trip, as a matter of fact."

"So, what did you come up with? Did you decide on doing anything differently? Did you think of any way you could stay home more?"

126

Before he could respond, Karen asked in a half whisper, "Did you talk to Mary Ann yet? You know, concerning who we talked about before?"

On her way to the living room with the drinks, Mary Ann heard Karen.

"WHO did you talk to Thomas about before?" Mary Ann asked.

"Oh, no one, dear, it's not important. We don't have to talk about it now."

"Look, both of you," Thomas said sternly. "I've only been home a few minutes. I haven't talked to Mary Ann about anything, and I haven't decided anything. But, I think there is more going on around here than I know about."

The children were coming down the stairs now, making their way to sit and have a nice visit with their grandparents, when their mother said, "No Karen. I do think it's important. Who did you talk to Thomas about?"

The children were instantly on edge and knew something bad was about to happen.

"Well... someone named Reggie," Karen said.

"OH, MY GOD! Karen! Are you kidding me? That was a private conversation! You don't know what you're talking about!" Mary Ann exclaimed.

"Well, then, I'd like to know how I was wrong," said Karen.

"Hold it," Rich said. "This is none of our business. Besides, the kids don't need to hear any of this."

"Be quiet," Thomas said to his father. "Mary Ann, you were telling me something about Reggie when I got home."

Thomas looked at her as if to ask if she may want to tell him something now.

"Are you OUT OF YOUR MIND?" she said. "Those two things have absolutely nothing to do with each other."

"I doubt that," Karen said just barely loud enough to be heard.

"Now, that's ENOUGH!" Rich said loudly.

Mary Ann thought Rich was about to defend her to his wife, but all he said was, "What's this all about, Thomas? Have you and your mother been discussing something?"

"I don't think—" Karen began.

Thomas cut her off and looked at Mary Ann with concerned, soulful eyes and asked, "I just have to know, Mary Ann. Are you going to ask me for a divorce?"

"WHAT?" everyone yelled at the same time. "Where did you get that idea?" Mary Ann asked as she shot Karen a dirty look.

Jenny jumped to her feet and shouted, "LEAVE MY MOM ALONE! She was just in a car accident and almost died!"

"WHAT?" everyone yelled again.

Now the whole room was in an uproar, with everyone staring at Jenny. She and all four grown-ups were all talking at once. Michael and Todd looked at each other with eyebrows raised, not knowing what to do or say.

"HOW could you possibly know that, Jennifer?" Mary Ann asked in astonishment.

"So, it's TRUE?" Thomas shouted. "You almost DIED?"

The uproar continued. All the grown-ups were firing off a barrage of questions when Todd stood up and said, "Please... stop."

The questions continued from all sides.

"NO ONE told ME you were in an accident? When did this happen?" Rich asked.

"WHERE did you get the idea that I wanted a DIVORCE?" Mary Ann said.

"Everybody, please stop. I have something to say," Todd said a bit louder. But no one paid any attention to him.

"Oh, my God! Were you hurt?" Thomas asked.

"I'm sorry I said anything to Thomas," Karen told Mary Ann. She then turned right around and asked Jenny, "Where did you hear about the car accident dear?"

"I said SHUT UP!" Todd yelled. NOW he had their attention. "SIT DOWN, all of you, and BE QUIET!"

Todd had gone to the dining room table and was in full view of everyone in the adjoining room. He was standing on a chair on the far side of the dining room table, looking almost like a young man on a stage with all four chairs on that side of the table pulled out and pushed next to each other. He paced back and forth on them, like a General addressing his troops.

"NOW, I'm going to tell you all something, and I don't want any interruptions until I'm finished. Do you copy?"

He looked right at Grandpa Rich, who just sat there with his eyes and his mouth wide open.

"Ahhh... yeah... copy, Cap... I mean, Toddy." Grandpa Rich said.

"Okay," Todd began. "For weeks now, Dad, I've been trying to tell you about something amazing going on with me, but you NEVER listened.

Well, you're GONNA listen now! First of all, I've been trying to tell you about Sparky coming to me in my dreams. Well, they're not just dreams... they're real. And he's real."

"Now, come on, Toddy, Sparky died... a long time ago," Thomas said.

"You'll get your turn to talk," Todd said. "But not right now. I don't know how to explain it, so I'll just tell you what I know."

With everyone's full attention, Todd calmly began as he walked from chair to chair without looking at them. "When Sparky first came to me, he just showed me a few things that didn't really mean much at the time. I told you about them, too... four boys swimming in a river, a boy and his dad building a house. I tried to tell you about them, remember, Dad?"

"Yes, I remember," Thomas replied sheepishly.

"Well, that was YOU, Dad, and YOU, Grandpa Rich!"

"Oh, my gosh! How do you know for sure?" asked Thomas.

"I'm going to tell you. For starters, Sparky showed me things that happened a long time ago, things I didn't know anything about. But then, he showed me things about Michael and Jenny. So, I told them about Sparky and that I thought he was real. Well, they just laughed at me. They told me I was stupid to believe that a dog in a dream could know anything about anything. That is, until I had a dream about each of them. I saw Michael at school and Jenny at the mall with her friends. I told them again. I told them everything that happened in the dream. They said that it was exactly what happened to them the day before."

Michael and Jenny both nodded their heads in agreement.

"But, they still didn't quite believe me," Todd said. "Michael wanted to know who I had spyin' on him."

Michael smiled and nodded again.

"But then, one night Sparky came to all of us, one by one. He brought us through this tunnel kind of thing. When we went out the other end, we all ended up in the same dream."

"What the heck do you make of this, Thomas? Are we going to have to take him to some kind of specialist?" Rich asked.

"Shhh... He's telling the truth," Jenny said. "That's how we knew you were in a car accident, Mom, and we can prove it. You were driving down State Street. All three of us were in the back seat. I mean, in our dream we were in the back seat. Anyway, I think you were upset. The light turned yellow and you didn't even slow down. It turned red and we heard a loud horn blaring. Then a big pickup truck roared by, right in front of you and splashed water on your windshield."

Mary Ann sat totally dumbfounded, staring at her daughter who was recounting exactly what had happened to her earlier that month.

"Oh, honey, I almost lost you," Thomas said.

"Michael tried to tell her the light was changing, but she couldn't hear him," Jenny added helpfully. "Then the car spun around, slammed into the curb, and you were facing backward in the street."

"Good Lord, Mary Ann. Is that REALLY what happened?" Rich asked as Mary Ann sat staring blankly, nodding slightly in agreement.

"Why didn't you tell me about the accident?" Thomas said again, watching Mary Ann.

"I don't know. It just didn't seem important after it was over... I was alright and the car was alright."

"Did you ever tell YOUR mom about YOUR accident?" Todd asked his dad, with a little tilt of his head.

"What accident?" Thomas asked his young son.

"The one when you were a boy about Michael's age, and your friend Mike fell through the ice, and you jumped in to save him."

"How in the WORLD?" Thomas exclaimed.

"WHAT?" Grandma Karen said. "You fell in that icy river and NEVER told me?"

"HOW IN THE WORLD could you KNOW THAT?" Thomas asked in shock.

"Thomas, ANSWER me!" Karen said. "You fell in that icy river? Why didn't you ever tell us?"

"All four of us promised not to tell because we were afraid you wouldn't let us go hunting together after that," Thomas explained.

"Well, Grandma, hold on to your knickers," Todd said, "because he didn't just jump into the icy river. They both went down and couldn't get back out. So, they swam downstream under the ice and tried to come up in a totally different spot, but they couldn't quite break through. Thankfully, Sparky could tell where they were and started barking and biting and scratching at the ice so the other two boys would come and help."

"Is this TRUE, Thomas?" Karen asked in a panic.

Now Thomas was nodding blankly and marveling at Todd.

"So, Mike was a pretty important person to you, wasn't he, Dad?" Todd asked.

"Yes," Thomas replied. "I never had a brother, but I'd have to say that

Mike was just like a brother... I loved him like a brother. He's who you're named after, Michael."

"Do you remember what he said to you after you guys brought him back with mouth-to-mouth resuscitation?" Todd asked.

"OH, MY GOD!" Karen cried out. "HE WAS DEAD?" Thomas Richard Preston! You mean to tell me a boy actually DIED and NOT ONE OF YOU thought it might be IMPORTANT ENOUGH to tell us... or tell his parents, or take him to the doctor!?"

"Mom, we were about 15 years old... we didn't want to get in trouble." Thomas said. "Besides, that was like, 30 years ago. You're going to yell at me NOW?"

"I DON'T believe it. I just DON'T believe it," Karen shrieked as she pulled her knees up to her chest, wrapping her arms around them. She sat blankly on the couch and rocked back and forth in her seat, imagining all the terrible ways that this story could have gone.

"I do remember what Mike said to me after we brought him back. He said I didn't quit on him. I jumped in to help him, so he wasn't going to quit on me," Thomas said.

"You don't like the idea of quitting very much, do you, Dad?"

"No, I hate it. I can't stand the idea of being a quitter," he said.

"I know. I think we've all heard you say it, like a million times, but do you really think he meant plain old quitting, to just stop doing something? Or, do you think he meant quitting on something important, like someone you love... quitting on a member of the family?" Todd asked.

Thomas looked at Todd in complete amazement, like someone had just switched on a light.

"I'll be damned," he said. "I haven't thought about it in a long time, but I'm sure you're exactly right."

"Mike wouldn't care if we quit a game or quit hunting to do something different. I'm sure he meant he wouldn't quit on someone he loved."

Thomas sat thinking about this to himself for about two seconds before Todd started in again.

"Another thing, Dad, you owe Michael an apology. You were yelling at him about fighting at school when you were on the phone, and you were sure that he was guilty of something—but he wasn't!" Todd said. "He was standing up to some boys who were trying to make him smoke marijuana! He couldn't tell YOU because I was standing right there. He didn't even try to defend himself because he didn't want to talk about marijuana in front of me."

"Is this true, Michael?" Thomas asked.

Michael nodded.

"Michael, I'm sorry. I really do owe you an apology," Thomas said. "Don't worry, I'll talk to someone at the school and get this taken care of."

"I'm not worried. It's already done. I'll fill you in later. But right now, I think Todd has more to say," Michael said.

"That's right I do. Now guess what? We're back to you, Grandpa," Todd smiled.

"Me? What did I do? What do ya need to bring me into this for?"

"Because, Grandpa, the most important dream is about you!" Todd said.

Grandpa Rich gave him a quizzical look.

"Okay, Grandpa, Michael and I were wondering how we would know when we become men."

"Well, I'll be," Grandpa Rich said. "The Captain—Uncle Doug's speech!"

Thomas sat up quickly and blurted out, "I remember that speech! The what-kind-of-man-are-you-gonna-be speech!"

"That's the one," Todd said.

"But it wasn't just Captain Doug's speech that was good. You had a pretty good one yourself, Grandpa," Todd said.

"I did? What did I say?" Rich asked.

"When Dad asked you if he was a man yet, you didn't laugh at him or anything like that. You stopped what you were doing, and you told him face to face."

Then Thomas spoke, repeating what his father said that day—years ago.

"Well, buddy, right now, you are more of a man than an awful lot of grown-up males I know. You give me a good day's work, you don't complain too much, you take responsibility for your mistakes, you're respectful of me and you're willing to do what it takes to make a better place for this family. Then you said that it was those things that made me a man. I'd like to think I still do those things today," Thomas said.

"Oh, Thomas," Rich said. "You remembered all that from all those years ago? Those are all fine things and you are a good man. But, when I said those things to you, I just wanted you to understand that work isn't anything to be afraid of. I wanted you to know how good it feels to accomplish a goal. I wanted to give you some skills that would help you all throughout your life, and I wanted you to know that you could have a little fun while doing it. Do you understand?"

Thomas nodded. "I think I got stuck on that part about accomplishing goals and forgot about the rest, huh? We did have fun building that cabin, didn't we, Dad?" Thomas asked.

"We sure did, buddy. And it was a fine cabin, don't ya think?"

"I certainly do. I remember how Sparky used to ride in the front end of that fishing boat with us. His front paws on the bow, his ears blowing out away from his head, flowing in the breeze with every little motion of the boat… I sure loved that dog," he added.

Thomas looked around and all the adults had tears in their eyes, but the three Preston children were just beaming at him.

"Why are you all grinning?" he asked.

"We saw all of this just a few of nights ago! I really liked watching you and Grandpa work on the cabin, Daddy," Jenny said. "It made us so glad to be part of the Preston family, right guys?" The boys nodded. "We all laughed when you kept tapping Grandpa's cap down with the toe of your shoe."

"Yeah. And he was trying to hold the ladder so tight so you wouldn't fall. He didn't realize you were fine and doing it on purpose the whole time," Michael said.

Rich and Thomas looked at each other, both saying at the same time, "I'd forgotten all about that!"

"There's something else, too, Dad," Todd began. "There's something very important in becoming a man, especially if you're going to be a man with kids someday."

"Oh? And what's that, Toddy?" Thomas asked.

"It's that you had a good example of how to be a great dad. We all thought so... Sparky included. Grandpa Rich was a great example for you. He was patient, caring, mindful of your feelings, and he was a good teacher."

"Oh, Sparky included, eh? What makes you think so?" Thomas asked.

"Yeah, I don't know how to explain it. I can't read his mind or anything, but I can tell how he feels about things."

"Grandpa Rich, he felt you were a great dad!"

"Well, how about that," Grandpa Rich said smiling and looking around at everyone. "I always knew that dog had superior intelligence. Ha, huh, huh," he laughed.

"Yes, Dad, you're a very good example," Thomas said sarcastically.

"I've got a question, Todd. Why didn't Sparky just come straight to me in MY dreams? Why do you think he went through you and your dreams?"

"I don't know. Do you think you would have thought he was real?"

"I don't know, buddy. Probably not," Thomas said after thinking about it a moment.

"I think maybe you had some things turned around in your brain so that some of those lessons you learned in the past weren't the same as you are remembering them now. Do you think that could be right, Dad?" Todd asked.

"Toddy, with everything that you've told us and shown us tonight, I'm sure you are exactly right. I think I became so focused on my own goals, that I just sort of made all those other lessons fit into place the way I wanted them to instead of really thinking about it like I should have. I'm sorry, everyone. I didn't mean to be so selfish. I just thought I was working hard for the family."

"Daddy, whatever happened to Mike Tise, the boy who almost drowned? I've never heard you talk about him," Jenny said.

"Well, Mike lives in Alaska in a little town called Homer. He and his family moved up there shortly after he graduated from high school. Mike teaches biology and works with the Alaska Fish and Game Department studying the local halibut, a flat fish that everyone likes to catch up there. Mike studies their habits, keeps track of the numbers of them caught and their sizes, and things like that. Then the Fish and Game Department can adjust the fishing season accordingly."

"Do you ever see him anymore, Dad?" Jenny asked.

"No... not in a long time. But we still talk on the phone three or four times a year. He's still one of my best friends, and I still can't think of anyone else I'd rather have you grow up to be like, Michael."

"Does he have any kids?" Jenny asked.

"He has a daughter named Anna and a son... a son named Thomas," Thomas said.

Mary Ann smiled.

"You never told me that," Karen said.

Thomas smiled a little and shrugged, "That was between him and me."

"I think it's love," Rich said to no one in particular.

"What do you mean, Grandpa? What's love?" Todd asked.

"Well, buddy, this whole thing... Sparky coming to you and showing you things about his family after all these years. I think love is the most powerful thing in the world... and I think that the love your dad and Sparky had for each other when your dad was a young boy was a special thing."

"Now, I might be wrong, but YOU are a part of your dad. Heck, you even look like him when he was your age. I think maybe that's why Sparky chose you to come back to, Toddy. He felt that same love with you that he had with your dad all those years ago."

"I think you're right, Grandpa. Sparky wanted us to know how special our family is and why. To know about our past, our love for each other, what it might be like if one of us was gone. He wanted us to work together to SEE it—Michael, Jenny, and me. He wanted us to know that we all need to work together to KEEP it, to not be so selfish and do everything on our own all the time. That's why he came to me—to us."

Once again, they were all quiet for some time, contemplating the theory of Sparky's return.

"Toddy, will you do me a favor?" Thomas asked.

"Sure, Dad."

"The next time you see Sparky, tell him thank you, and that... I love him," Thomas said as his eyes went glassy.

Both Grandma Karen and Mary Ann let out an "Awwww" at the same time.

"Well, I can tell I've got a lot of thinking to do here in the next week or two," Thomas stood up and said. "But first, I'd like to talk with my wife and see if we can come to some kind of understanding about what's going on around here and what we might have to do next."

"Come on, Karen. Let's leave these people alone. I'm sure they've got a lot to talk about, Rich said, turning toward Todd. "Young man, well done," Grandpa Rich said, patting Todd on the back.

After a bit of small talk with Mary Ann and Thomas, Grandpa Rich and Grandma Karen made their way to the door. Rich offered his hand to Thomas, who grabbed it and shook it firmly, then gave his father a big bear hug and said, "Thanks, Dad."

"What for?" Rich asked.

"For everything."

"You're welcome," he said, shaking his head at Thomas. "That's the craziest damn thing I ever heard tell of... a dog coming back to life in a dream. That's one for the books!"

Mary Ann and Grandma Karen hugged, too. "I'm sorry, too, dear," Karen said, taking hold of both Mary Ann's hands. "I'm sorry I jumped to conclusions about you and this Reggie person. You know I've always thought you were the perfect person for my son. And I still do. But when I overheard that conversation, something inside me snapped. I guess after I heard it, the momma bear in me came out and I just didn't know what to do about it. So, before you judge me too harshly, do me a favor: Ask yourself what you would do if it was you and you'd heard Michael's wife say those things accidentally? I love you, dear, and I hope you can understand my position."

Mary Ann smiled as they both hugged again before Rich and Karen headed down the sidewalk to their car.

Mary Ann turned her attention toward her children, acknowledging what they'd been through in their dreams with Sparky.

"There's just one more thing I'd like you kids to do for me now," she said. "Go upstairs and do your homework, and let me talk to your father alone." Mary Ann smiled sweetly at them. They knew everything was going to be all right.

Thomas and Mary Ann sat down across from each other at the kitchen table, agreeing it had been quite a night.

"Look, Mary Ann. We never did get to finish our discussion from before. I know you were apprehensive and concerned about how I would react to what you had to say, but I know it's important to you, and I'd like to hear it, if it's alright with you. Was any of what my mom said true?"

"It was all true," Mary Ann replied.

Thomas' eyebrows lifted in surprise, and he felt that pain in his stomach coming back.

"But none of it is what she thought, or what she made you think. What I was trying to tell you was that Reggie and I were working that night and everything was just so perfect."

Thomas gave her a very serious look of concern.

"Just wait," she said reassuringly. "It was the perfect escape... the Danforth Parlor, the candlelit room, the wonderful smell of Peking Duck, the wine ... all of it. I felt like I was transported to another place and time. I was special, like a princess or some aristocrat from the 1920s having a lovely meal in my fabulous home. And then... he kissed me... or I kissed him."

"WHAT?" Thomas said.

"Well, we shared a kiss and that's what I felt so guilty about. And THAT'S what I couldn't tell you on the phone. Oh, Thomas, the instant it happened it was like all that fantasy disappeared and I was just me again. It was almost like a punch in the stomach, kind of a rude awakening. I pushed him away and grabbed my purse and ran to my car. I was so confused and hurt and ashamed. I didn't want to be in that situation, and I wanted someone to blame... Reggie, the wine, YOU, anyone but myself. I didn't want to hurt Reggie either. He and I have been friends for a long time and I really don't want to lose that. He's smart and funny, too."

"Okay... okay," Thomas said.

"No... I mean too, like also. You are smart and funny and so is he. Oh, Thomas, if you are going to forgive me, you need to know for what... right? I spent a lot of time going over it in my mind, but I couldn't come to grips with it until I finally admitted to myself that I was to blame, too. I was a mess, and then... that's when the accident happened... exactly like Jenny said it did. Except she didn't mention that I found an empty parking lot, parked the car and just sobbed for about half an hour."

"My gosh, honey, I'm sorry that happened to you."

Thomas reached across the table and held her hand. "I could have lost you. WE could have lost you!"

Mary Ann squeezed his hand a little.

"So, what did my mom hear that was wrong?" Thomas asked.

"Okay, first tell me exactly what she said," Mary Ann requested.

Thomas began, "Ah... okay, she said she heard you say no to Reggie, and that you couldn't talk right now, and that it wouldn't happen again, and that you and he just can't do that."

Mary Ann slowly began to smile. "Alright," she said. "When I answered the phone, he asked if he could talk to me. I said *no* because your folks were here, and I was still a little irritated with him. He started apologizing, like I hadn't just told him I couldn't talk right now. Then he started talking about the art show and if I knew that they weren't going to let the hotdog guy from Oakbrook in so we wouldn't have a repeat of what happened last year. But I already knew that. So, I said, *I know, it won't happen again.*"

Mary Ann started to giggle a little.

"Then, when I said, *We just can't do that*, he said that the crew from the Porta Potty Company wanted to know if they could wait and pick up the units on Tuesday. Well, we have a contract with them and the city, and they had already agreed to pick them up on Monday. So I said, *We just can't do that!*" She was laughing harder now.

Thomas began to laugh, too. "So, you're telling me that I worried

141

myself sick over Porta Potties?"

Mary Ann had both hands covering her mouth as she laughed and nodded yes to his question. Thomas shook his head.

"I can't believe it. I flew home early, certain that you were going to divorce me, all because of Porta Potties!"

Thomas thought for a moment. "Wait a minute," he said. "What about the hole in your life. My mother mentioned that, too?"

Mary Ann stopped laughing. "You know, I've been meaning to talk to you about that, too," she said. "I've been thinking about it constantly ever since I mentioned it to your folks. The hole in my life is YOU."

"WHAT?"

"It's YOU, Thomas... It's the fact that you're not here. You're my husband, my partner and friend. I love you. I miss you when you're gone, and more than that, I need you. I need you to be here with me... and the kids need you, too. Thomas, you're a good man. You're smart, you're funny, you have a great heart and the kids need to see that... to see you more often. Remember what Todd said? To be a good man, a boy needs a good example."

Thomas looked down a little and nodded in agreement.

"So, you'll try? Will you do that for us?"

Thomas nodded again and said, "I'll see what I can do." Then, with a smile, he said, "Wait till I tell my mom I almost got divorced over Porta Potties!"

Mary Ann laughed and said, "Ohhhh! Could you do me a favor and not tell her anything for a week or so? I want her to sweat a little for starting this whole thing."

"Okay, deal. I won't mention it for a week. But, what are you going to do about Reggie? I mean, seriously, how do you feel about the man? Have you talked to him at all yet?"

Mary Ann looked Thomas straight in the eyes. "Thomas, I'm not going to lie to you. I like Reggie very much. He's one of my oldest and best friends. We have a lot in common. He's smart and funny and, well, he's not hard to look at, and—"

"Alright, alright, I get it! GEEZ!" Thomas said.

"Anyway, Thomas, there's nothing wrong with Reggie, except for the fact that he's not YOU... and I want you. I learned that for sure that night, too!"

"So... what are you going to tell Reggie?" Thomas asked.

"Well, I guess pretty much what I just told you. I'm going to tell him that he is one of my best friends and I don't want to lose that. I'll tell him that's all we can be, and if that's okay with him, then we can go right back to being friends. I'll tell him that I'll listen to anything that he would like to say, and then we aren't EVER going to talk about it again. If that's not good enough, then I guess we can't be friends anymore because no good can come of it."

"Well, that's pretty good... I guess," Thomas said, looking down at the table with a kind of a pouty frown on his face.

"What else is there to say, Thomas?" Mary Ann asked, truly concerned.

"Well... you could tell HIM the part about how you love ME, and how I'M smart, and funny, and how I'M not hard to look at and—"

"Yes, yes, Thomas. You're very cute! I'll be sure to tell him."

"And the other stuff, too?" Thomas asked.

"Yes... the other stuff, too," Mary Ann said through a smile. "Geez, you can always make me smile, you big jerk," she said, pushing his hands away, still smiling.

# 11

Thomas tossed and turned in his bed that night and woke up early the next morning, staring at the ceiling and thinking about his schedule at work for the next couple of weeks. Though it was pretty light, the events of last evening weighed heavy on him. Now, laying the ground work for his own presentation, he began reviewing his notes and rereading everything he had researched on the computer before writing down his final set of notes that outlined putting his plan into action.

For the next two weeks, he kept himself very busy. He was attentive to the kids, showing interest in their activities as he clearly tried to make up for lost time. Still, he was constantly on the phone and on the computer, always writing things down in a notebook and drawing sketches for some kind of a plan, like a blueprint for a carpenter. Whenever anyone would ask what he was doing, Thomas would simply smile and say, "I'm working on my presentation." This drew tremendous groans from everyone in the family until they finally had enough.

"Seriously?" Jenny said to her mother. She was the first to complain about their father and another presentation.

"Gosh, Mom," Michael said. "Didn't he learn anything from all we told him? All that we saw with Sparky? Your accident? I mean, come on!"

Todd saw a change but not what he expected. "He sure seems happy and he does do a lot more stuff with us," he told his mother. "But he's still working awful hard, too. I asked him what he was doing and he just said he's working on his presentation. But he looks at me like he has a secret or something."

"Alright, that's it," Mary Ann said. "I'll talk to him, Toddy. Go get your brother and sister and bring them back here."

"Thomas!" Mary Ann called out. "Thomas! I'd like to see you for a minute."

Thomas came in from the garage. "Yes dear, what is it?" He smiled and tried to kiss her on the cheek, but she pulled away looking cross.

"What's going on?" she asked.

"Why, honey?" Thomas said, blinking in an exaggerated way, like a cartoon character. "Whatever do you mean?" he said like a kid with a good report card who was going to spring it on his parents at the last minute.

"Alright, what are you up to?" she said, arms folded across her chest. "The kids want to know, too."

"Well then, I guess it's time to show them and you what's been going on. I'll see you all in the family room in five minutes. Trust me."

Thomas kissed her on the cheek without giving her a chance to back away this time.

Five minutes later he came clamoring into the family room with his laptop, some large cardboard charts, an easel to set them on and a yardstick. Everyone looked around at each other. *What the heck is this?* they wondered.

145

"First of all, I'd like to thank you all for coming," Thomas began, speaking in his most professional voice. "I'm sure some of you are wondering why I called you all here today."

Mary Ann rolled her eyes. Todd giggled and looked hopefully at his father, as if he was about to learn a great secret.

"Thomas, what is this?" Mary Ann asked.

"Why, it's my presentation, my dear," Thomas replied. With his laptop set up for a PowerPoint presentation, Thomas dimmed the lights. "Now, many of you know me, but for those of you who don't, I'm Thomas Preston, and I'll be delivering the presentation this afternoon."

"OH, FOR CRYING OUT LOUD!" Mary Ann said. "Just get on with it!"

"Oooh... rough crowd! At any rate, you'll see by my first graph that this is the average number of days per month that I'm normally gone out of town on business. Now, as you can see by this next graph, the number-one thing I'd like you to notice is that the average number of days per month drops from seventeen days to one. This is due to... MY NEW JOB! I will only be required to do one, three-day seminar every three months!"

"Oh, my gosh, Thomas, are you serious?" Mary Ann asked with elation.

"That's fantastic, Daddy!" Jenny shouted.

Todd and Michael just smiled at each other.

"I know you've all been very patient with me, and I want you to know I appreciate it very much," Thomas said. "So, anyway, you guys sit down. There's more. I went to my boss and told him I had an idea for the company. Not that my goal was to stay home more... but I had done my homework and showed him how much money could be generated by the last idea I had. You know... the one about the monitoring device with the monthly fees."

Mary Ann nodded along with the children.

"So, I told him what I would like to do is give these seminars once per quarter to people in the gas industry to generate interest in our new product. I explained how quickly the numbers multiplied by having our customers on a monthly retainer. Obviously, the more customers we sign up, the faster that happens. He was all ears, and that's when I told him I was so excited about this, that I wanted to work on it full-time from this local office. I told him I'd like to be in charge of coordinating research and development with the sales staff, instruct them on how it works, and how to present it to new clients. Well, the long and short of it is that he thought it was a fantastic idea, and that we should implement it immediately, and that I will start out at my current salary—plus commissions on new business—and 1000 shares of company stock."

"Thomas, that's WONDERFUL!" Mary Ann said excitedly.

"Yeah, I think so, too. I'll have an office here in town, so I'll be home every night AND every weekend."

"Wow! I can't believe it!" Mary Ann said as she got up and hugged her husband.

Michael, Todd and Jenny gathered around him, too, and gave him a big family hug.

*******

The following weeks brought many good times and many more wonderful things to the Preston family. Thomas had forgotten how much he enjoyed just talking to his children, learning what they found fun and interesting. When talking to Michael about his music he'd say, "Show me how you write a song," or "Read me something from your notebook." He'd ask Jenny who Megan was seeing these days, and if she was going out for the school play this year. He was genuinely interested in what she had to say.

Jenny made good on her promise to Megan, too. She took everything they had stolen back to the store in the mall and asked to see the manager. The young clerk at the counter went to the doorway at the back and asked the manager, Connie Davis, if she would come out and talk to this young lady.

When Connie came out she saw Jenny standing sheepishly next to the sales counter with a brown paper bag in her hands from one of the local grocery stores.

"May I help you?" she asked Jenny, who simply looked down into the bag and said, "Yes—I took these things from your store without paying, and I'm very sorry. I would like to return them. I understand if you need to call the police, my parents, or whatever. But I feel very guilty about it. and I'm here to make it right."

Connie Davis was speechless. She had never in her six years as manager had anyone bring back stolen merchandise before. She stood and looked at Jenny for what seemed like forever.

"You'd better come with me," she said.

Connie took Jenny into the back room through a narrow hallway of

stacked boxes and into a small office where she asked her to take a seat. She gestured to a metal folding chair next to a little wooden desk. Jenny sat while Connie stood, and looked at her again without saying a word as she sized up Jenny.

"Your parents don't know you're here—is that right?"

"That's right." Jenny replied.

Connie gave her another long stare. "Look at you," she said. "You're nicely dressed, your hair is done well, you're cute. I'm pretty sure that either you or your parents could afford to buy you these things. So, why did you steal them?"

Jenny thought for a moment. "I just wanted to be like the other girls, the cool girls, and I didn't want my parents to know."

"But you're alright with me calling them now?"

Jenny looked up at Connie, then back down at her knees and shook her head. "Yes."

Connie looked at her again, silent for a long moment. When Jenny looked up, Connie was smiling.

"Umm... why are you smiling?" Jenny asked.

"Because... you remind me of me," Connie said. "When I was just a little older than you, something very similar happened to me. Only I didn't have the guts to return the items I had taken. That decision haunted me for a long time after that."

"Because you felt guilty?" Jenny asked.

"I did," Connie replied. "So now, this is what I've decided to do with you."

Connie took out a small notebook from the desk drawer. "What's your name?"

"Jenny Preston."

Connie scribbled in the notebook.

"How old are you?"

"I'm almost fourteen," Jenny answered.

"What are your parents' names?" Connie asked.

"Mary Ann and Thomas Preston," Jenny replied.

"How are your grades?" Connie asked.

"Mostly *As* and *Bs*. Why?"

"I'll ask the questions, thank you very much," Connie said. "Have you ever done anything like this before?"

"No, never," Jenny said.

More scribbles from Connie.

"And if I talk to your guidance counselor at school, he'll tell me the same thing?"

"Ah, yeah, I think so."

"What's your counselor's name?"

"Mr. Bentendorf."

"Have you learned anything from all this?" Connie asked.

"Yeah, I learned to be honest with my *real* friends and ask for their *opinions* before I volunteer them for anything."

"Would you like to know what I learned when it happened to me?" Connie asked.

"Uh, sure," Jenny said, feeling like she really didn't have any choice in the matter.

"I learned that I couldn't control what anyone else thought about ME. I could only control what I thought about ME. That, my dear, has helped me a great deal in the time since. Okay, one last question: Do you think you might like to work here when you get a little older?"

"What? Are you kidding me? Sure! You guys have all the coolest stuff and the best sense of fashion design, and… seriously? You would really consider hiring me?"

"I would," Connie said. "It took a lot of courage for you to come here today, especially without a parent. Now, you know you shouldn't have taken those things in the first place, but you came here on your own to correct your mistake, so I think you must be more honest than not. Would you agree?"

Jenny nodded.

"I wish I'd had your strength when it happened to me. I could have put that haunting guilt away a lot sooner. Anyway, here's my deal," Connie said. "If you can stay out of trouble and keep your grades up, you can come and see me when you turn sixteen, and I'll give you a try. Deal?"

Jenny's eyes were wide open. She stared at Connie with a slight tilt to her head, trying to process what she had just heard. Then, as if she just suddenly realized what Connie meant, she asked, "You mean, I can GO?"

Connie smiled and said, "You can go. But remember, I've got my eye on you, young lady," and she waved her little notebook at her.

Jenny left the store feeling absolutely wonderful. She couldn't wait to tell Megan. She also couldn't wait to tell Todd that she had returned everything—and what had happened at the store with Connie.

# 12

Thomas and Todd really had great fun in the weeks since Sparky's visit, though Thomas had more than one surprise in store for his young son. First of all, those carpenter blueprints he'd been working on were plans for a tree house for Todd. Thomas had made many additions and changes on them in the last week but finally decided it was time to unveil them. When he showed the real plans to Todd, he was ecstatic about the idea. He could hardly control himself.

"Oh, Dad, this is gonna be awesome!" he said.

"And, we're going to build it together," Thomas said. "Michael, I want you to help, too."

Michael liked the idea very much. He thought back to the dream where he watched his father and grandfather working on the cabin. "Yeah, that'll be cool with me," he said.

Thomas went over the plans with Todd to make sure that everything would be just right. "Now listen, Todd, if there's something that you don't like, or if you want to put something in that I don't have yet, let me know okay?"

"Okay, Dad."

They talked about trapdoors and fire poles and things like that. This was the most fun Todd ever had. Together, they finalized the plans for the tree house and a couple days later, Thomas had some lumber delivered so they could get started.

They were supposed to start on Friday afternoon when Thomas got home from work. Todd could hardly contain himself as he arrived home from school. He went to the garage and gathered up every tool he could think of that might be needed for the project, put them in his wagon and brought them out by the pile of lumber. He removed the tarp from the lumber and began placing the tools in neat rows so his father could see them easily.

When Thomas got home that afternoon, he didn't look very happy.

"I'm all ready, Dad... ready to start on the tree house," Todd said with a bright smile on his face.

"Well, I'm not so sure that's going to happen, not tonight at least," said Thomas.

"What's wrong, Dad? Are you okay?"

"Yeah, I'm fine, but something happened on my way home from work and... well, I'm just not sure you're gonna want to do any building once you hear about it."

"Well, what is it?" Todd asked.

"Before I tell you, is everyone home right now?"

"Yeah, everyone is inside."

"Okay," Thomas said. "Why don't you run and get them. That way, I can tell you all at the same time and I won't have to repeat myself, alright?"

"Ahh... sure," Todd said as he ran off to get the rest of his family. *This must be terrible,* he thought. *What kind of awful news could this be?*

Todd returned a few minutes later with the rest of the family, all quite concerned about what kind of misfortune was about to fall on them.

"What's going on, Dad?" Michael inquired.

"Oh, I was explaining to Todd that something happened to me on my way home tonight, and after he found out what it was, he probably wasn't going to want to work on the tree house. I just thought it would be best to tell you all at the same time."

"What is it, Thomas? What happened?" Mary Ann asked.

"It's a funny thing... I was on my way here and my car just started turning all by itself, taking me down roads I've never been on before," Thomas explained. "Well, suddenly it stopped and I found myself at the hospital."

"The hospital!" Jenny exclaimed.

"Yes, the animal hospital, where I met this little dog that wanted to come home with me."

Thomas opened the back hatch of his car, and out jumped a small black and white puppy.

Todd was instantly in love with the part Border Collie and part Golden Retriever that tumbled out and fell on his little snout. He didn't look anything like Sparky, who was mostly Beagle, but he was black and white and very cute.

"Oh, Thomas, he's adorable," Mary Ann said. "What's his name?"

"Well, that's a good question. He doesn't have one yet. I thought the kids could name him."

"Oh, that's a wonderful idea! I think they should!" Mary Ann said.

Todd was already rolling around in the grass with the dog when Thomas asked, "How bout it Todd? You ready to start on the tree house?"

Todd was still snuggling with the puppy when he looked up at his dad.

"Ah, maybe we can start it tomorrow?"

"That's what I thought, too," Thomas said.

*******

For the next two weeks, the boys worked on the tree house, and they all worked on training the puppy. Things had never been happier at the Preston household. Grandpa Rich and Grandma Karen got to meet the new puppy and they, too, fell instantly in love with him.

"What did you come up with for a name, Toddy?" asked Grandpa Rich. "Sparky Junior? Sparky the Second?"

"No," Todd said, "His name is Topr."

"Topper? Like T-O-P-P-E-R?" Rich asked.

"No. Topr. That's T-O-P-R," Todd said. "It's the first two letters in Todd and the first two letters in Preston. Michael thought of it. Pretty cool, huh?"

"I think that's a fine name. You guys all did a great job."

The whole family talked and laughed and had a wonderful visit and a really nice evening together, and when it was time to leave, Rich took Thomas aside and said, "I'm really proud of you son, I mean it. The way you got your boss to see things your way, the way you work and play with these kids, it's great! I've not seen YOU this happy in a long time."

"Thanks, Dad. You were right about so much. I don't even know where to begin. I'm still amazed that, to help me see things clearly, it took my childhood dog returning to this family through my children's dreams!"

"Yes, that's an incredible story, and one incredible little dog," Rich said, giving Thomas a hug as they said their goodbyes for the night.

*******

It had been almost four weeks since Todd, Jenny, and Michael told their family about the dog and the dreams that changed their lives. Since that time, neither Todd nor Jenny nor Michael had another dream about Sparky. Jenny and Michael didn't think much about it. Their lives were full and rich right now, with many things to occupy their minds. But Todd often thought about Sparky, his father's stories, and the way he felt when he was with the little black and white dog... and that night, before he went to sleep, Todd had hoped that he could dream about Sparky one last time—but he didn't.

The next day, Todd and his father were working with Topr, training him to walk close beside them when he was on the leash... to stop when they said *stop* and things like that. They had walked a long way already and were near the park on Hilltop Drive, when Todd saw something ahead. Sitting in the grass, just off the sidewalk, about a block away, was Sparky.

"Dad, look!" he said in almost a whisper, not sure of what he was seeing, and desperately wanting his father to see the same thing.

"Dad," Todd said again, "That's Sparky!"

Thomas looked where Todd was pointing and said, "Sparky?"

The two looked at each other for a moment.

"SPARKY!" they both shouted, running up the hill towards the little black and white dog with Topr in tow.

As they got closer, Sparky stood up and happily wagged his tail as they approached.

"Come on, Dad, that's him!" Todd said.

They ran faster, with the little dog turning slightly and walking casually over the hill with his white-tipped tail still wagging happily behind him. When Todd and his father reached the top of the hill, they jogged to the place where Sparky had been just a second earlier. He was gone. There was nothing but a wide-open park with freshly mowed grass. There were no bushes or flowers in which to hide. Sparky had disappeared.

Todd and Thomas looked at each other in disbelief. "I know it was him, Dad. I just saw him. I SAW HIM RIGHT THERE!" Todd said, visibly upset as he pointed to the spot where they had last seen their Sparky.

"I know, son, I know... I saw him, too!"

"It was Sparky, wasn't it, Dad?"

"It sure was, Todd," Thomas said smiling at his young son. "I know my own dog when I see him."

"Well, where is he? Why did he disappear?" Todd asked.

"I don't know, buddy, I don't know."

They stood there in silence for some time, looking and watching to see if Sparky would return. Finally, Thomas said, "I guess he just knew that his job was done—and that we're gonna be okay."

# EPILOGUE

Todd and Thomas walked home slowly without saying much of anything until, finally, Thomas said, "Gee, Toddy, I really wanted to see him one more time." Todd nodded, and that was it. They were so disappointed, they didn't know what to say. But, as they walked home with Topr by their side playfully nipping at the leash from time to time, their mood slowly brightened, and without a word, father and son walked quietly, watching this new little dog that was simply being himself—so happy to be there with his new masters.

As they continued along the path, Thomas put his arm around Todd's shoulder, and they both smiled. Thomas realized that even though he was disappointed about Sparky, he really had everything he needed all along. His family was happy, his children were close now, and this new dog would make new memories for his children to share. He and Mary Ann were close now, too.

Thomas went to bed that night feeling happy. As he thought about the choices and changes he'd made over the last few weeks before he drifted off to sleep, he was feeling good about his family and this new home that he was a very big part of now. Then suddenly, he was greeted by a small black and white dog that he knew at once was Sparky!

The dog jumped into his arms and licked his face the way he'd done so many years ago. Thomas was young again.

Without hesitation, he ran with Sparky to play in a field on the grassy hill near the cabin he and his father had built. It was a wonderful dream. And the only person Thomas ever told about it was Todd.

# ABOUT THE AUTHOR

Dan Grunwald is a lifelong artist and jeweler, as well as storyteller, dog lover and family man. After graduating from St. Cloud State University in 1981 with a degree in fine arts, he began working part time in the jewelry business for Bachman Jewelers in St. Cloud, Minnesota. Before fulfilling his dream of starting his own jewelry business in 1991, he learned a great deal working with the jewelers and goldsmiths at CJ's Jewelers in Oklahoma City, Oklahoma, as well as Stadheim Jewelers in Albert Lea, Minnesota, where he worked for seven years as lead goldsmith.

Today, Dan is still successfully running and growing his business, Grunwald & Kiger, with his partner Jaimi Kiger. In addition to making and selling jewelry, Dan enjoys all kinds of art forms, from sculpting and pottery to drawing and painting. (He has recently picked up the brushes again to create a new series of watercolors.) His writing has been inspired by the countless books he read to his children when they were young, as well as his desire to share some important life lessons with them in a fun and interesting way. Dan lives with his wife Judy in Ventura, Iowa. *A DOG'S TALE: Sparky Rescues the Prestons* is his first book.

# ACKNOWLEDGMENTS

Thanks to Dawn Bassett, Michelle Penning and Jules Hermes for their editing skills.

Thanks to Mike Kraemer, Nick Brascugli, Mark Schorn, Gloria Fennell, Joel Clancy and Joette (Jet) Kofoot for previewing this book and providing me with your helpful critiques and encouragement.

Thanks to all the teachers who read and reviewed this story: Terri Siguenza, Sharon Tarr, Karen Stephany, Nancy Tovar, Cathrine Peterson, Jim Hardwig, and Janet Boehnke. Your wisdom and expertise about stories for children in this age group is greatly appreciated.

Also, thanks to Hannah Blaha and Hunter Nielson, my two young beta readers who provided excellent feedback and age-appropriate insight.

A special thanks to my family, friends and coaches who have shaped my thinking on what is important in life. Through their thoughts, actions and experiences, they have had an influence in who I turned out to be.

And a BIG thank you to Captain George Clements, the real Captain who gave a group of Boy Scouts and myself a very concise talk about what to do and not to do in life as you learn who you are and who you want to be. In chapter 8, Captain George's speech is given by Captain Doug, named after my respected uncle.

# HOW TO USE THIS BOOK

*For Teachers and Parents*

Topics for discussion in the classroom and at home:

- Sibling rivalry
- Manipulative people
- Bullying
- Code of Honor
- Peer pressure
- Selfishness
- Setting goals
- Defining success
- Home
- Family
- Responsibility
- Apologies - parents and kids
- Family loyalty
- Trustworthiness
- What it means to face consequences
- Goodness (something good coming from a bad situation)
- Drugs and people who sell them
- Stories of past pets
- Carelessness
- You and your future
- Moving on from disappointment
- Making good choices
- What parents want for their kids
- Forgiveness
- Deciding to focus on what YOU think of you

*To contact Dan Grunwald, visit: www.grunwaldoriginals.com, or visit: www.sparkyrescuestheprestons.com.*

Made in the USA
Coppell, TX
18 April 2020